D0766928

"And would you not be believin' your own eyes, then, lass?"

Sabrina glared at the now visible Fergus. "You switched the cookie plates! Aunt Hilda wouldn't have deliberately sent the real shamrock cookies to Mr. Kraft."

"Aye, and I did."

"Don't I get three wishes or something?" Mr. Kraft asked. He was remarkably calm, under the circumstances.

"Only if you catch one of the wee folk, which you didn't. However, would you be interested in findin' the pot of gold at the end of the rainbow?" A cloud of golden dust swirled through the room as Fergus waved his hand.

The mortals gasped in awe as the end of a glorious rainbow suddenly filled the far side of the room.

Sabrina groaned.

Titles in SABRINA, THE TEENAGE WITCH™
Pocket Books series:

All Pocket Books titles are available by post from:
**Simon & Schuster Cash Sales, P.O. Box 29, Douglas, Isle of Man
IM99 1BQ**
Credit cards accepted. Please telephone 01624 675137,
Fax 01624 670923, Internet http://www.bookpost.co.uk
or email: bookshop@enterprise.net for details

Sabrina ☆ The Teenage Witch™

Shamrock Shenanigans

Diana G. Gallagher

Based on Characters Appearing in Archie Comics

And based upon the television series
Sabrina, The Teenage Witch
Created for television by Nell Scovell
Developed for television by Jonathan Schmock

POCKET
BOOKS

LONDON · SYDNEY · NEW YORK · TOKYO · SINGAPORE · TORONTO

POCKET
BOOKS

An imprint of Simon & Schuster UK Ltd
Africa House, 64-78 Kingsway
London WC2B 6AH

Copyright © 1999 Viacom International Inc.
All rights reserved.
POCKET BOOKS and colophon are registered
trademarks of Simon & Schuster
A CIP catalogue record for this book is
available from the British Library

ISBN 0 671 02937 1

1 3 5 7 9 10 8 6 4 2

Printed by Caledonian International
Book Manufacturing, Glasgow

For my Irish husband,
Marty Burke,
with love and affection always

Shamrock Shenanigans

☆

Chapter 1

☆

Sabrina Spellman crept out her bedroom door and across the hall, groping for the banister in the dark. Curling her hand over the railing, she moved to the head of the stairs and paused. An uneasy quiet filled the house.

Had she dreamed the clattering noise that had awakened her? Shrugging, Sabrina turned to go back to bed. Something fuzzy brushed her bare leg.

"Sleepwalking or testing a night vision spell?"

"Salem!" Startled, Sabrina's hand shot to her chest. "I thought I heard something downstairs."

"Some*thing* as opposed to some*one?*" Salem lowered his voice.

"Like rattling pots and pans," Sabrina whispered.

A scraping noise rose from the kitchen.

1

"It's probably just Hilda rummaging around for a late-night snack," Salem said softly.

Sabrina cautiously moved down a couple steps and leaned over the banister. No light shone from the kitchen. "In the dark?"

"The refrigerator lights up when you open the door. Unfortunately, *I* can't open the door when I get the midnight munchies," Salem muttered. "I have to rip open cereal boxes with my bare teeth."

"Aunt Hilda doesn't have to rummage if she gets hungry. She can just order from Other Realm Point-out." Sabrina glanced down. She could just barely make out the cat's form in the predawn darkness. "And Presto Pizza has twenty-four-hour linen closet delivery."

"Then who or *what* is in the kitchen?" Salem's voice quivered slightly.

"That's what we're going to find out."

"We?" Salem balked as Sabrina tiptoed down the stairs. "I may be a cat with a weakness for chasing things that roll, fly, or scamper, but I *don't* do things that go bump in the night."

"I've got a magic finger, remember?" Sabrina whispered over her shoulder.

"Oh, yeah! Pity the poor prowler. *If* it's just a prowler." Salem sighed. "Isn't this the scene in horror movies where you always complain about the stupidity of the character who goes to investigate?"

Sabrina paused. *"They* can't turn an intruder

2

into a mouse and send in the family cat to corner it," she pointed out.

"Oh. Well, in that case, I'll go first. Having acute night vision hardly offsets the disadvantages of being a cat, but we might as well make the most of it." Salem trotted past Sabrina on silent feline pads.

"After you." Sabrina continued her descent and winced when a stair creaked underfoot. In the glow of the porch light shining through the window by the door, she saw Salem freeze on the foyer floor. The cat graced her with a look of arrogant feline disdain.

"Why don't you just zap up a bullhorn and announce our imminent arrival?" he hissed.

"Sorry." Sabrina waved the cat on. Her bare feet made no sound on the wood floor as she followed his dark silhouette through the living room. Salem paused at the kitchen doorway, tail twitching in apprehensive anticipation. Sabrina shivered in the eerie silence, raised her finger, and nodded at the cat.

As Salem assumed pounce position, the kitchen lights suddenly flashed on. With a screeching yowl, he leaped into the room.

Surprised, Sabrina fired off a wild point and shouted, "Freeze!"

Simultaneously Aunt Hilda jumped up from the floor by the table and pointed from the hip. "Gotcha—" She froze.

A large net hovering near the ceiling dropped over Sabrina.

Salem skidded to a halt on the linoleum and gawked. "Uh-oh. I think we're in trouble."

"No, we're not. Aunt Hilda won't blame me for turning her into an icicle. I thought she was a burglar." Moving slowly and deliberately, Sabrina squatted and slipped her hands under the edge of the net so she wouldn't get hopelessly tangled.

"I'm not worried about Hilda," Salem said shakily. "I'm worried about *what* she was expecting to come through the door! That's a big net!"

"We're in trouble!" Sabrina squealed as the net suddenly tightened around her wrists and ankles, then *whooshed* upward. Dangling in midair with her fingers and toes aimed at the ceiling, she glanced at Aunt Hilda, whose face had been flash-frozen in a moment of maniacal glee. Her aunt was also wearing a combat helmet, elbow and knee pads, and a bandoleer stuffed with a variety of protective charms. Sabrina frowned, suddenly sharing Salem's concern. What exactly *had* Aunt Hilda been lying in wait to trap?

"Stay still!" Salem warned. "That's a boa net! The more you struggle, the tighter it'll get."

"Now you tell me." Sabrina looked down at the stricken cat. "Get on the table and jump to get me swinging, okay?"

"I don't think so. That net will snag anything

that touches it, and I am *so* not into spending the rest of the night as a piñata."

"Neither am I," Sabrina said patiently. "But unless I get my finger aimed at Aunt Hilda to unfreeze her, I'll be stuck until Aunt Zelda wakes up."

"I could go get her—" Hopping onto a chair, Salem cocked his head thoughtfully.

And something *thumped* in the living room.

"What was that?" Salem's fur stood straight up on his arched back.

"I don't know, but you'll have to slip past it to get Aunt Zelda. I'm sure you can handle it, Salem. Whatever it is." Sabrina paused to let the prospect of engaging the unknown, and possibly dangerous, intruder sink in, then offered an alternative. "Or you can swing me so I can point!"

"Okay, okay! Ready, aim"—Salem crouched, then launched himself at her—"fire!" The net constricted around his paws when he made contact.

As Salem's momentum and weight swung the net, Sabrina bent her finger toward her aunt. "Thaw!"

"—you little cheat!" Aunt Hilda started, then blinked when she saw Sabrina swinging in the net with attached cat. "What are you doing?"

"Oh, just hanging out." Sabrina grinned sheepishly.

"This is no time for games!" Eyes flashing, Hilda pointed and chanted.

"Release your prisoners, boa net,
and for that Fergus creep get set!"

The boa net instantly loosened, dumping Sabrina and Salem onto the mattress that Hilda quickly conjured to break their fall. Sabrina rolled off and Salem jumped aside. Aunt Hilda removed the mattress with another point as the net repositioned itself near the ceiling.

"I think my circulation has been permanently cut off." Salem moaned and vigorously rubbed his front paws together.

Sabrina slumped into a chair and dusted off her nightgown. "Who's Fergus?"

"The most ornery, cantankerous leprechaun I have *ever* had the misfortune to meet." Hilda huffed.

Sabrina looked up sharply. "This is March seventeenth."

"It is?" Salem perked up.

"Exactly. St. Patrick's Day." Frowning, Aunt Hilda inspected the boa net. "But this year it's D-Day for that no-good, rotten little chiseler."

"Looks to me as if you're the one expecting the invasion." Sabrina eyed the magical charms tucked into the loops on Aunt Hilda's bandoleer. She recognized several that were designed to ward off everything from swarms of buzzing bugs to itchy rashes and furniture fungus.

"That Irish twerp has been driving me crazy

with his pranks every St. Pat's Day for the past one hundred and twenty-five years."

"I didn't notice anything unusual last year," Sabrina said.

Hilda rolled her eyes. "Last year he locked me in my room with a TV that wouldn't turn off and only showed infomercials for weight-loss scams and gourmet dessert recipes."

"I rather enjoyed the time he filled the house with mice." Salem smiled.

"Not that you were much help, Salem." Hilda shuddered. "That was almost as bad as the year he sent a plague of door-to-door salesmen with buck teeth and bad breath and rigged the doorbell to play 'Finnegan's Wake' all the way through whenever it rang."

"'Whack to the doodle, dance with your partner,'" Salem sang in his deep baritone. "'Out to the floor ye—'"

"Salem!" Aunt Hilda snapped. "If you ever want to eat tuna again, cease and desist this instant!"

"'—trotters shake . . .'" Salem's voice trailed off.

"What did you do to Fergus to set him off, Aunt Hilda?" Sabrina asked.

"Nothing . . . *much.*" Aunt Hilda shrugged. "I just refused to pay him for a boot he made."

"Leprechauns are the finest shoemakers in the world," Salem said. "But they only make one. Never a pair."

"Except Fergus didn't tell me *that* when I placed my order!" Furious, Hilda flicked her finger. A forest green, high-heeled boot with a delicate swirling pattern in gold appeared in her hand.

"It's beautiful!" Sabrina exclaimed.

"It's a work of art," Hilda agreed. "But I've got *two* feet! So I'm not paying until he delivers the other one."

"And Fergus won't stop pestering her with pranks until she pays," Salem added.

"Don't take any bets on that. This year I'm gonna catch him and end it once and for all. One way or another." Grinning, Aunt Hilda pointed. A jug of hocus-pocus punch and two plates of cookies decorated with green icing shamrocks appeared on the table. "Maggie Phillips is out on maternity leave, and I've got an audition for her seat in the local orchestra this morning. Fergus is *not* going to ruin it."

Sabrina frowned, baffled. "You're gonna battle a leprechaun with punch and cookies?"

"Bait," Aunt Hilda explained. "Most leprechauns have a weakness for food and drink. Fergus can't resist punch and pastry."

Sabrina shook her head, amused by the image of a cranky, two-foot leprechaun with a sweet tooth.

"Cookies!" Salem dived for the nearest plate.

"Not those!" The cat flopped on the table as Aunt Hilda whipped the plate away. *"This* is the

Fergus batch, made with real shamrock. And you know what affect shamrock has on you, Salem."

"What affect?" Sabrina asked.

"Similar to catnip," Salem said. "Only I get totally mellow instead of super hyper."

"We found out the hard way that he's allergic." Hilda set the plate of real shamrock cookies at the far end of the table. She put the other plate in the middle. "Mice are not afraid of limp, mellow cats."

"But I *so* enjoyed watching you and Zelda spend the day leaping from one piece of furniture to another, trying to avoid them." Salem chuckled, then stopped when Hilda glared at him.

"Watch it, Salem!" She wagged a finger at Sabrina. "No real shamrock for Salem. Or for any mortals, either."

"What happens to mortals?" Intrigued, Sabrina leaned forward.

"Normally, no one can see the wee folk unless they decide to make themselves visible," Hilda said. "Real shamrock allows mortals to see the wee folk whether they want to be seen or not. And the faery people turn out in droves on St. Patrick's Day."

"What does shamrock do to witches?" Sabrina asked.

"Same thing, only witches don't freak out when they see a bunch of winged faeries and little bearded men in funny clothes having a high old time in their midst. Now—" Hilda adjusted her bandoleer. "If you don't mind, I've got a leprechaun to catch."

"Which worries me because I don't find that at all weird." Rising, Sabrina headed out the door. "Guess I'll go back to bed."

Grabbing one of the no-shamrock cookies in his teeth, Salem padded after Sabrina as Hilda switched off the lights.

Sabrina's eyes slowly adjusted to the gray light of dawn filtering through the windows. She didn't notice the cookie in the cat's mouth until he dashed ahead of her on the stairs. "I hope you're not planning to eat that in bed, Salem!"

"Ah unt 'eve a rum," the cat mumbled through his cookie-stuffed mouth.

"See that you don't. I hate crumbs in—" Sabrina stopped abruptly when a shrill shriek erupted from the kitchen.

Salem dropped the cookie. "Take cover! Fergus is back!"

Chapter 2

Sabrina spun around to return to the kitchen.

Salem stopped her with a claw in the hem of her nightgown. "Not a good idea. Innocent bystanders have been known to regret their proximity to ground zero and Fergus fallout."

A chair fell over, followed by a series of thumps, bumps, and unintelligible shouts.

"But it sounds as if the kitchen is getting the worst of it." Uncertain, Sabrina hesitated.

"What is going on down here?" Slipping into a robe, Aunt Zelda ran down the stairs.

"Well," Salem said dryly. "Either Hilda finally caught Fergus or the slippery Irish imp put one over on her again."

Glass shattered in the kitchen.

"Is it St. Patrick's Day again already?" Aunt Zelda slumped in exasperation. "Fergus may have a grudge against Hilda, but everyone in the house pays for it. We *still* have mice in the attic!"

"And you have no idea what a sense of security that gives me," the cat said.

"We have security mice?" Sabrina ducked as a pestle rocketed through the kitchen door and thumped against the far wall.

Salem flinched, then shrugged apologetically. "More like an anti-ennui cache. As long as those mice are in the attic, I know I'll never be bored."

Zelda glared at him. "In the meantime, the insulation is being shredded, and we've got holes in all the cereal boxes."

Having confessed to being the midnight mangler of helpless cereal boxes, Salem shot Sabrina a warning look. "Is it *my* fault life around here is never dull? Noooooo."

Another crash and more thumps were followed by a hysterical laugh.

"You'll not be holdin' me for long, Hildy!" A tenor voice shouted. "Mark me words, you won't."

"Wanna wager your gold on that, Fergus?" Hilda's shrill squeal rose above another series of loud thumps.

"That's it!" Throwing up her hands, Zelda picked up the pestle and stormed toward the kitchen. "I'm not spending another St. Patrick's Day worrying about being the victim of that leprechaun's practical jokes."

"Has that happened?" Sabrina asked Salem as they hurried after Zelda.

"Only if you count green hair dye in the shampoo or having 'Kiss me, I'm Irish' tattooed on your forehead."

Zelda stopped dead in the doorway. Sabrina peered over her shoulder. A very small, gray-bearded old man with pointed ears was tangled in the boa net on the floor. His green eyes glittered angrily under the brim of a squashed three-point hat.

The kitchen was a shambles. Broken dishes and glassware littered the floor. Two of the chairs had toppled, and the window curtain was torn. Boxes and canned goods had been flung haphazardly around the room. A can fell out of an open cabinet and rolled to a stop at Zelda's feet. Zelda picked it up, then stared at Hilda, who stood in the middle of the mess beside the angry, netted leprechaun.

"Look, Zelda! I got him!" Hilda beamed as she pushed her combat helmet up off her eyes. One knee in her pants was torn. The bandoleer had slipped off her shoulder and drooped around her waist. She kept it from falling with one hand.

"Sure and it's a bunch more trouble you'll be bringin' on yourself, Hildy," Fergus grumbled in a thick, Irish brogue. "And that's a promise I can keep with no trouble a'tall."

"Thank goodness!" Zelda flicked her finger.

"Kitchen trashed by Irish storm,
be gone the broken, tossed, and torn."

Broken glass disappeared. The fallen chairs righted themselves. New curtains appeared on the window, and everything that belonged in cabinets returned to them.

Salem sauntered over to the net and fixed the snagged little man with an unblinking stare. "I'd say 'top o' the morning' to you, Fergus, but looks to me as if Hilda's got the upper hand."

"Mind your tongue, cat, or I'll—" Fergus stuck a warning finger through the mesh. The net instantly clamped around it.

"Or you'll what?" Salem chuckled.

"I'll, I'll—take back the mice I left in the attic!" Fergus sputtered, his face reddening.

"I *so* wish you would," Zelda said with an annoyed glance at Fergus.

Sabrina sighed, certain that none of her friends would awaken to find a vindictive leprechaun trapped in their kitchen. Of course, none of them had an aunt who was a witch with a legitimate and unresolved customer complaint.

"Actually, Fergus," Hilda said, "you'll be too tied up today to do much of anything."

"What's that, you say?" Fergus frowned uncertainly. "Sure and you wouldn't be thinkin' o' keepin' me trapped in this net the day long, now would you, Hildy? It's St. Patty's Day!"

"Exactly!" Aunt Hilda smiled, then scowled. "And it's Hilda. Not Hildy."

"Isn't keeping him in that net all day a bit drastic?" Sabrina asked.

Aunt Zelda looked at her askance. "You wouldn't think so if you had danced a jig every time a colleague at M.I.T. said 'hello.'"

"And what were you doin' wearin' Hildy's shoes, I'd like to know?" Fergus asked. "The pixie happy-feet powder I sprinkled in them was meant for Hildy and not you, Zelda."

Hilda slipped off the bandoleer and dropped it on the island counter. "Speaking of shoes, Fergus—"

"I don't care to discuss it!"

"Fine." Folding her arms, Aunt Hilda shrugged. "Because *I* don't care if you spend your favorite holiday trussed up like a plucked chicken."

"I'd reconsider, Fergus." Sitting down at the table, Sabrina picked up a no-shamrock cookie.

"And who might you be?" Fergus asked warily.

"This is our niece, Fergus," Aunt Zelda said. "Sabrina."

"And you can take my word for it," Sabrina added. "I know that look. Aunt Hilda means what she says."

"Aye and that's the sad truth of it, lass." The leprechaun nodded. "She's as stubborn as an Irish drizzle, Hildy Spellman is. She never lets up."

"Look who's talking." Taking a seat beside

Sabrina, Zelda started the coffeemaker with a limp point.

"After a hundred and twenty-five years, I'd say Fergus and Hilda are evenly matched when it comes to being obstinate." Salem jumped onto the table.

"But not when it comes to wits!" Fergus huffed.

"I caught you, didn't I?" Aunt Hilda glared at the leprechaun. "So *you* have to grant *me* three wishes."

"Three wishes? Cool!" Sabrina grinned.

Salem's ears perked forward. "I wish for a never-ending smorgasbord of fresh fish, caviar, shrimp, tuna—mmphffff."

"Stuff it, Salem." Hilda shoved a cookie in the cat's mouth, then looked back at Fergus. "Before I let you go, I want your word of honor you won't disappear if I turn my back."

"Leprechauns can do that?" Sabrina asked. "Pop in and out like we do?"

Zelda nodded. "Yes. If you don't keep your eye on them, they can become invisible."

"Is that your first wish, Hildy?" Fergus cocked a hopeful eyebrow.

"No. That's the deal, if you want me to set you free before midnight," Hilda said.

"On my oath, then." Fergus mumbled without conviction. "I won't disappear until after I grant your wishes."

"Fair enough." Grinning, Hilda pointed. Fergus

unfolded on the floor as the net suddenly vanished.

"You trust him to keep his word?" Sabrina asked, aghast. Fergus shot her a disgusted look as he dusted off his crimson red jacket and green britches, then polished the silver buckles on his black leather shoes with his hand.

"Absolutely." Sitting down, Hilda pointed a thick cushion into the fourth chair and motioned Fergus to sit. "He may be short, but he's a Celt, and a Celt would rather die than break his given word."

"Another unfortunate truth." Fergus climbed onto the chair and helped himself to a shamrock cookie.

"So what are you going to wish for, Aunt Hilda?" Sabrina pointed up a glass of orange juice.

"How 'bout a heap—hic—o' raw oyster-errrs?" Salem swayed slightly.

Zelda gasped. "What kind of cookie did you just give him, Hilda?"

"Gooood cooook-ieee." Grinning foolishly, Salem barely stopped himself from falling over.

Hilda glanced at the plate of *real* shamrock cookies and grimaced. "Oops."

"When did we get a revolving kishhin?" Moaning, Salem keeled over and covered his eyes with his paws.

"Isn't there something we can do for him?" Sabrina winced in sympathy for the giddy Salem.

"I'm afraid not." Hilda sighed. "But don't worry. The effects will wear off in a few hours."

"Or you could *wish* the poor critter's shamrock stupor away," Fergus suggested coyly. He took a bite of his real shamrock cookie, then nodded with approval. "These are delicious, Hildy!"

"Actually, that's not a bad idea, Hilda." Zelda opened the dish cabinet with another casual point. "We can't just point it away. Salem's condition *is* your fault."

"That's right," Sabrina agreed. "It's not like he snitched the cookie. You gave it to him, Aunt Hilda."

"Oh, no." Hilda held up her hands and sat back. "I'm not wasting one of my wishes on—"

"Whaaaack to the dooodle, dance"—raising his head, Salem crooned the chorus of "Finnegan's Wake"—"wiiith yer partner—"

"Stop it, Salem," Hilda snapped.

"Out ta th' floor ye—hic—trotters shaaaake!" Salem's head lolled to one side, then snapped up. "Wassssn't it the trufff I tol' yaaaaaa—"

Sabrina cast a sidelong glance at Aunt Zelda, who was also trying not to laugh. Aunt Hilda covered her ears.

"Lotsa fun at Finn-in-inegan's—"

"I wish Salem was immune to the effects of real shamrock!" Hilda spat out the wish in a rush.

"Done!" Fergus snapped his fingers. A stream of glittering, golden dust whipped around the cat.

"Waaake—" Salem blinked.

"How do you feel, Salem?" Sabrina asked.

Salem coughed. "A little dry. Got milk?"

"And I'll be havin' a wee bit o' that hokie-pokie brew, Hildy." Fergus grinned.

"It's hocus-pocus punch. Don't look so smug, Fergus." Hilda frowned as she pointed a glass into the leprechaun's hand and poured. "I've still got two wishes left. And I *really* wish you'd stop calling me Hildy!"

"Done!" Laughing, Fergus snapped his fingers. The glittering gold dust whisked around his head. "And what'll you be havin' for your third wish, Hilda?"

Hilda stared at him. "You tricked me!"

"Now, Hild*a.*" The leprechaun's green eyes twinkled with mischievous delight. "Sure and you should know by now that *no one* can outwit a leprechaun."

Furious, Hilda glared at the wizened little man. "Is that so?"

Sabrina sipped her orange juice, kept quiet, and took mental notes. She had almost had to marry Roland the troll because she had signed a contract without reading it. She didn't want to risk making a similar mistake with a leprechaun out of ignorance. Especially since Roland was a pint-sized Prince Charming compared to the ornery Fergus.

"More punch, please." Fergus held out his glass.

"I'm going to make my third wish now," Hilda said flatly.

"Milk!" Salem gagged.

"Sorry, Salem." Zelda yawned as she zapped up Salem's bowl on the island counter. Then she turned her finger to the stacks of coffee cups and mugs in the cabinet.

"And are you sure you wouldn't want t'be thinkin' about that third wish for a while?" Fergus asked Hilda.

"No." Hilda started to pour punch into the leprechaun's glass. "I wish for you, Fergus the leprechaun, to make the *left* foot boot to match the *right* foot boot I got from you one hundred and twenty-five years ago, and you will do it before midnight tonight."

"Done," Fergus mumbled, then snorted as another swirl of golden dust encircled him.

"Good." Hilda sagged with obvious relief. "Then I'll pay you and we'll be even."

"Aye, but it's a sorry thing to be wishin' a leprechaun to defy *centuries* of tradition."

Hilda eyed the dejected-looking leprechaun curiously. "Worse than asking where your pot of gold is hidden?"

"Well, no—"

"Too bad."

"Where's my favorite mug?" Lowering her finger, Zelda went to the cabinet and began shuffling through the rows of coffee mugs by hand.

"Yeow!" Salem howled. "Oh, gag, yuck! Pifff-tuy!"

Sabrina glanced at the cat in alarm.

Hissing and spitting, Salem turned in frantic circles on the counter. "Sour! The milk is sour!"

Startled, Hilda sloshed punch on the leprechaun's coat sleeve. "Wha—"

"Watch it now, Hilda!" Ignoring the cat, Fergus jerked his arm back. "I just had this coat cleaned for the St. Patty's festivities!"

"Fergus!" Zelda turned away from the cabinet, her eyes flashing. "Isn't it bad enough that we have to deal with your pranks every year? Did you *have* to sour the milk, too?"

"I'm a leprechaun! What do you expect? Souring milk and hiding things is written right into our job description." Fergus brushed golden dust off the shoulders of his jacket. The glittering sparkles settled over the cookie plates.

"Where's my coffee mug?" Zelda kept her gaze fastened on the leprechaun.

"Your mug?" Squinting thoughtfully, Fergus pulled on his beard. "Well, now, if I took it—and I'm not sayin' I did—I might have stuck it in that drawer behind you, Zelda."

"Nice try, Fergus," Zelda said, "but I'm *not* taking my eyes off you until I've got my mug back."

"And how are you gonna to be after findin' your mug if you won't look for it?" Fergus chuckled.

Annoyed by the leprechaun's condescending tone, Sabrina blurted out what she was thinking without thinking. "For a cute, little short guy, you sure don't worry about who you insult, do you?"

"Cute!" Fergus banged his glass down on the table.

"Oh, boy," Salem muttered. "Now you've done it, Sabrina."

"Done what?" Bewildered, Sabrina started as the leprechaun jumped on the table and shook his finger in her face.

"You'll not be insultin' me and get away with it!" Drawing himself up to his full two-foot height, Fergus stamped his foot in a petulant rage. "Take it back!"

Hilda leaned over and whispered. "Take it back, Sabrina. Leprechauns hate to be ridiculed, and they've gotten a lot more sensitive since St. Patrick's Day became another commercial holiday gold mine."

"With good reason!" Fergus huffed, his green eyes flaring with indignation. "All those cards and posters with happy-go-lucky leprechauns on them have totally ruined our image!"

"It's a major improvement, if you ask me!" Rising, Sabrina planted her hands on her hips and matched his stubborn glare. She really didn't think the scrawny, wrinkled, and cantankerous Fergus was cute, but she wasn't going to give him the satisfaction of saying so.

"You'll be havin' nothing but trouble until you learn some respect, Sabrina Spellman." Snatching his flattened hat from his head, Fergus dropped it on the table, stepped on it, and began to spin.

Trouble? Sabrina wondered. *What kind of trouble?*

Getting dizzy as Fergus became a whirling blur, Sabrina looked away. Apparently, so did Hilda, Zelda, and Salem. When she looked back, the leprechaun was gone.

Chapter 3

☆

"Salem, have you seen my other brown suede ankle boot?" Wearing the left boot, Sabrina hobbled to the bed and looked under it. No right foot boot.

"Can't say that I have." Salem licked his paw and gave his face a quick wipe, then stretched out and yawned. "If I can't eat it or chase it, I don't keep track of it. It's a cat thing."

"I had both of them yesterday!" Frustrated, Sabrina threw up her hands and sat down on the bed beside Salem. She shot back up to her feet when the mattress made a loud, disgusting sound. "Did my bed just belch?"

"If my ears aren't deceiving me, yes. It did."

"Funny. I don't remember feeding it." Running late, Sabrina kicked off her single boot and pointed on a new pair. However, the cream color of the zapped boots didn't complement her beige boot-cut leggings and forest green mesh shirt over a green camisole as well as the darker real ones. "Maybe Libby won't notice."

"You think?" Salem asked sarcastically.

"No. Libby can spot a speck of lint at fifty yards, but I don't have time to worry about being fodder for her daily fashion review." Sabrina flung her backpack onto the bed and began stuffing it with books and papers. "Where's my red spiral notebook?"

"Unless it sprouted legs and ran away from home, it's probably still on your desk. Where you left it last night." Salem moaned as Sabrina rushed to the desk. "Would you mind pointing up a dish of tuna? I need it to get the taste of rotten milk out of my mouth."

"Gosh, Salem. My finger's fresh out of tuna. How about a nice dose of peppermint-flavored cat treats?" Sabrina shuffled through the papers on top of the desk, but the missing notebook with her history homework wasn't there. She opened the desk drawer and shrieked. It was full of small green snakes.

"Aw, come on! My breath isn't *that* bad—" Salem arched his back and hissed as a mass of harmless grass reptiles slithered out of the drawer and onto the floor.

The bed burped when Sabrina jumped onto it. "Snakes. I hate snakes!"

Someone laughed.

"Okay! Who's the wise guy?"

"Have a guess." Fergus suddenly appeared sitting on the turret windowsill. He tipped his hat and winked. "That's a grand trick, now, isn't it, lass?"

"You!" Sabrina glowered at the smiling imp. "Why don't you take your tricks, your snakes, and yourself back to Ireland where you belong!"

"Didn't you know?" Fergus teased in his lilting tenor. "There be no snakes in Ireland."

"Right. St. Patrick drove them out in the fifth century. So take a hint and get them out of my bedroom!"

"Well, actually, St. Patrick had naught to do with the lack of snakes in Ireland." Fergus cocked his head and tugged on his pointed ear. "There were no snakes on the Emerald Isle to begin with."

"There wasn't a snake social going on in my desk, either!" Sabrina shuddered as Salem took a flying leap off the bed into the squirming mass of reptiles—

"Wahoo!"

—that had suddenly turned into a pile of crimped crepe paper snakes.

Salem batted one of the fake snakes across the room, then pounced after it.

"Had you goin' there, didn't I?" Laughing uproariously, Fergus slapped his knobby knee.

"Very funny." Stepping off the bed, Sabrina eyed the leprechaun warily. "Did you hide my boot and my homework? And give my bed a bad case of indigestion?"

"Now, *why* would I be tellin' you if I had?"

Sabrina raised her finger. "So I don't turn you into a cute little leprechaun lapel pin?"

"A more terrible fate I couldn't imagine." Fergus nodded soberly, then chuckled. "But your magic won't be workin' on me today."

"Really? My finger was working just fine a few minutes ago." Sabrina pointed at her head. The sides of her blond hair were instantly pinned back with little green shamrock-shaped sparkly barettes. "Still does."

"But not on me," Fergus said confidently. "I cursed you first."

Salem looked up suddenly with a paper snake clamped in his teeth.

"Curse?" Sabrina started. "Wait a minute. You don't mean that thing you said about having trouble, do you?"

"That's exactly what I meant. So"—Fergus jumped from the windowsill onto the chair and struck a cocky pose—"my magic negates your magic until the curse is satisfied."

"Which will be when?" Sabrina asked with a pained smile.

"When you honestly respect me and not one second sooner!" Throwing out his chest, Fergus waved his hand with a flourish.

"That long, huh?" Nibbling her lip, Sabrina

took a step and stumbled. Her boot laces had been tied together.

Salem dropped the paper snake. "If it's okay with you, Sabrina, I think I'll hang out in Zelda's room until you and Fergus settle the score."

"Thanks a lot, Salem. I thought only rats deserted a sinking ship!"

"And cats who value steady nerves. Fergus only plagues Hilda one day a year, and my diminishing tolerance for unexpected surprises has almost ruined Christmas!"

"Wait a minute, Salem. There's got to be—" As Sabrina bent over to untie the knot in her laces, she heard a tearing sound. "Oh, no. Please tell me I didn't just rip the seat of my pants!"

"You didn't just rip the seat of your pants," Salem and Fergus said in unison.

"No, really." Standing up, Sabrina glanced over her shoulder. "Did I?"

"No," Salem said. "Witch's honor. Cat's honor. Whatever applies."

"You're no fun a'tall, cat!" Fergus tossed a torn sheet of paper over his shoulder. It vanished with a soft *pop.*

Relieved, Sabrina retied her boots, then straightened up. Fergus was staring at her and stroking his wispy gray beard. "What?"

Fergus smiled slyly. "Oh, I was just thinkin' . . ."

"Time!" Making the classic time-out sign with her hands, Sabrina started to sit on the bed, then sank onto the silent settee at the foot of it instead. "Okay, Fergus."

Salem sat by the door, curious but ready to bolt.

"Yes?" The leprechaun popped out with a twinkling of golden dust. He popped back in perched on a giant toadstool in front of her.

Coughing, Sabrina waved the dust away, then smiled. She didn't know how Aunt Hilda had survived one hundred and twenty-five years of the nasty leprechaun's St. Patrick's Day pranks, but she was absolutely certain she'd go nuts within the hour if they didn't stop.

"I just want you to know that—I respect you, Fergus."

"Witch's honor?"

"Uh—" Sabrina winced. She didn't dare swear on her witch's honor without really meaning it. She didn't know what the penalty would be, but it was sure to be worse than the wizened little man's practical jokes.

"Well, I can honestly say that I really don't think you're cute. You're scrawny, pinched-faced, and totally cranky. In fact, if you were any crankier, we could wind something up with you!"

"True, but beside the point," Fergus said. "Truth be known, it's not likely you'll ever be respectin' the likes of me, will you?"

Sabrina sighed. "Truth be known? Probably not. I mean, how can I honestly respect anyone who thinks it's funny to give a bed gas?"

"Well, then—" Fergus sighed heavily. "There's naught to be done for it except—"

"Exit stage right!" Salem pawed at the closed door.

"Except what?" Sabrina asked suspiciously.

"I don't supposed you'd be after doin' me a wee favor in exchange for liftin' me curse, now, would you?"

"That depends." Crossing her arms, Sabrina frowned. "What favor?"

"You steal the king of the leprechaun's gold, and I'll take back me curse."

"Gold?" Salem looked back just as the door swung open. "Did you say 'gold'?"

"You're kidding, right?" Sabrina blinked. "You're not kidding."

"A leprechaun *never* jokes about gold." The little man's brow furrowed. "It's not the spendin' of it, mind you, but the havin' it."

"What good is gold if you don't spend it?" Salem jumped on the bed. The bed hiccuped.

"'Tis the measure of a wee man's status, it is!" Green eyes gleaming, Fergus rubbed his gnarly hands together. "There be no finer sight in all the world than the sparklin' of gold!"

"And just where am I supposed to find the king's gold?" Sabrina asked.

"At the end of the rainbow," Fergus scoffed. "Where else would King Kevin be keepin' it?"

"The rainbow?" Sabrina laughed, then stopped

when the leprechaun shot her a warning look. "Sorry. What's the catch?"

"Catch?" Fergus blinked innocently. "It's an even trade I'm proposin', lass. No catch—"

"Unless King Kevin catches you," Salem said. "In which case, you'll be a captive in Faery Hill and in servitude to him for all eternity."

Fergus indignantly planted his hands on his hips. "You're lookin' to spend all eternity as a cottage doorstop, aren't you, cat?"

"Aunt Hilda was right, Fergus." Sabrina fumed. "You are a no-good little cheat. You didn't tell her you wouldn't make two boots. And you weren't going to tell me about the consequences of getting caught robbing King Kevin, were you?"

"I don't see that it matters." Fergus shrugged. "Given your total lack of respect, Sabrina, I'd be seriously considerin' takin' me up on my offer."

"I don't think so," Sabrina said.

"I would," Salem muttered. "A pot of gold would buy a lifetime supply of fresh fish."

To make his point, Fergus snapped his fingers.

A halo of golden dust appeared over Sabrina's head, then drifted down around her, transforming her into a giant magnet. She squealed as paper clips, pens, and miscellaneous jewelry flew off the desk and plastered themselves to her shirt, sweater, and pants. "Hey! I called time-out!"

"Aye and you did. My mistake." Fergus snapped his fingers again. Paper clips, pens, and jewelry fell to the floor around Sabrina's feet. "Now would you be takin' me up on my offer?"

Sabrina had no intention of striking a bargain with the leprechaun, but she grabbed the opportunity to postpone his pranks until she found another way to break the curse. "Can I think about it for a while? *Without* being distracted by any more tricks?"

"Fair enough." Jumping to his feet, Fergus grinned. "I'll get back to you shortly."

"How long—"

Fergus and his toadstool vanished.

Rolling her eyes, Sabrina grabbed the red spiral notebook that just as suddenly appeared on the desk, then changed into her real boots, which had also been returned. At least Fergus was putting his pranks on hold as promised.

"So when do we leave?" Salem asked eagerly.

"I'm leaving for school now. You're not going anywhere."

"I meant when are we leaving to steal King Kevin's gold?" Salem padded over to Sabrina's backpack. "Seems to me the risk of getting caught and enslaved by King Kevin is worth taking if that will get Fergus off your back."

"Not!" Shaking her head, Sabrina went to her dresser and rummaged through the top drawer. "I think I'll take my chances with Fergus. There's got to be a way to beat him at his own game, Salem. Aunt Hilda did."

"She caught him," Salem said. "And it took her

a century to do it. Catching a leprechaun and outsmarting one are two different things."

"We'll see." Sabrina slipped on her watch, then snatched her backpack off the bed. "Later, Salem!"

Salem didn't answer, but she thought she heard Fergus chuckle.

Chapter 4

☆

Have you seen Salem, Hilda?" Zelda walked into the living room as Hilda closed the fastenings on her violin case.

"Who?" Hilda took in several quick breaths, then breathed out slowly.

"The mailman."

"No. I haven't seen the mailman since the day I put the junk mail instant return charm in the mailbox. How was I supposed to know every advertisement he had delivered for the past month would *whoosh* back into his carrier bag all at once?" Closing her eyes, Hilda raised her hands, wiggled her fingers, then laced her fingers together and cracked her knuckles.

Zelda winced. Hilda was more nervous than usual about her audition for the vacated seat in the Westbridge Symphony. If she got it, the position would only last until Maggie Phillips returned from maternity leave in three months, but the additional performance credit would look great on her résumé.

"Calm down, Hilda. You're going to do fine."

"I'm calm." Hilda's hands shook as she shuffled her music sheets together and shoved them into a slim briefcase. "Who am I kidding? I'm about as calm as a clam sitting by a pot of boiling water."

"Well, at least you don't have to worry about Fergus playing any pranks on you today."

"I know, but it's really weird." Slipping a coat over her dark green tailored suit, Hilda scowled. "I've gotten so used to being on edge waiting for that puny Irishman to strike, being a nervous wreck on St. Pat's Day has become a habit."

"Yeah. I know what you mean." Zelda quickly scanned the room. "Every time I go through a door, I expect to get doused with a bucket of green oatmeal."

"Having green vegetable oil spray out of the shower was worse." Hilda picked up her violin and briefcase. "I'm going to be late if I don't get going. The city's already cordoned off the streets for the parade this afternoon, and this conductor despises tardy musicians."

"I forgot about the parade!" Zelda grinned. "And since we don't have to worry about what Fergus might do to spoil it for everyone this year, we should go. We could even do the town and celebrate tonight, too! A little corned beef and cabbage, some Irish music—"

"No, thanks. I don't do Irish music anymore. Listening to fifty renditions of 'Finnegan's Wake' pushed me over my tolerance limit. Which reminds me—" Hilda looked at Zelda pleadingly. "I need a huge favor."

"Does it involve dying anything green? Or inadvertently eating anything disgusting?" Zelda grimaced, remembering the green beetles Fergus had substituted for the walnuts in her Waldorf salad one St. Patrick's Day a few years back.

"No. Just take that plate of no-shamrock cookies over to Willard for me, will you? As a peace offering." Hilda headed toward the front door.

"Are you two fighting again?" Zelda sighed. Hilda and Mr. Kraft, the vice-principal at Westbridge High, had a stormy on-again off-again relationship that was almost impossible to track. Zelda didn't try unless their current romantic status was pertinent to the moment.

"No. Sort of. Yes!" Hilda paused with her hand on the knob. "He asked me to do *him* a huge favor tonight, and I had to refuse."

"What did he want you to do?" Zelda asked, curious.

"If I told you, you wouldn't believe it." Holding up crossed fingers, Hilda fled out the door.

Shrugging, Zelda pointed to change from her casual jeans and shirt into dark brown pants with a forest green blazer over an eggshell white blouse. As long as she was going out, it wouldn't hurt to get into the spirit of the Irish holiday. She added a green carnation to her lapel as she headed into the kitchen for the cookies.

Both plates were still on the table. And none of the cookies had kitty bite marks in them.

"Odd." Zelda frowned as she picked up the plate of no-shamrock cookies from the middle of the table. She hadn't seen Salem since he had gone upstairs with Sabrina, and it wasn't like him to ignore unguarded treats. Maybe the effects of the shamrock he had ingested earlier hadn't totally worn off and he was napping longer than usual.

Shrugging, Zelda covered the cookie plate with plastic wrap and carried it out to her car. For the first time since St. Patrick's Day had become a national event in the United States, she was free of Fergus to enjoy it.

"Hey!" Valerie intercepted Sabrina as she hurried to her locker. Dressed in dark green jeans, a short matching denim jacket, and green turtleneck, Sabrina's best friend gushed an Irish greeting. *"Dia duit,* Sabrina. It's a grand day, isn't it?"

"That depends on your definition." Sabrina fell into step beside Val. "By my definition, this St. Pat's Day is already whacked beyond salvaging."

Val's smile was replaced by a distressed pout. "But the day hasn't even begun, yet. What could possibly have gone wrong so early? I mean, I totally get into St. Patrick's Day, and I don't want *anything* to bum me out."

"Your last name is Birckhead, Val. That's not Irish, is it?"

"No. But that doesn't matter. Everybody's Irish today." She paused, then panicked. "Right? It doesn't matter, does it? 'Cause I can't go home and change. When did everyone decide to boycott St. Patty's Day? Why wasn't I told? Why—"

"Relax, Val." Sabrina calmed her paranoid friend. "You're just like everyone else today. I *promise.*"

"Oh, good." Val shrugged, then frowned. "So what's the problem?"

Sabrina hesitated, then decided to tell the preposterous truth. "Well, it all started when my aunt trapped a grouchy leprechaun in the kitchen because he owes her a boot—"

Val laughed. "Man, I'm so glad you were just putting me on! It's really a relief to know that someone else gets swept up in all this Irish stuff as much as I do."

"More like bulldozed in by a politically incorrect slip of the tongue." Sabrina shifted her backpack to her other shoulder. It seemed heavier than usual. "Leprechauns are not the easiest people in the world to get along with. They're *way* over the top when it comes to sensitivity issues."

"That's hard to believe. They look like such cute and carefree little fellas." Val paused, frowning again. "How come leprechauns are all guys anyway?"

"Maybe because girls aren't focused on hoarding gold, playing practical jokes, and cheating their shoe customers for fun and profit." Spotting Harvey walking toward them, Sabrina tried to change the subject. "Everyone seems to be getting into the spirit of the day. Hi, Harvey."

"Top o' the morning!" Grinning, Harvey Kinkle stopped in front of them. The words *Irish for the Day* were embroidered in gold on his green sweatshirt.

Val, however, was locked onto her train of thought. "So where do leprechauns come from then?"

"Ireland?" Harvey squinted, as though he thought it might be a trick question.

"What difference does it make?" Sabrina snapped without meaning to, then started when Fergus popped into the middle of the circle. Harvey and Val didn't react. Apparently, the leprechaun was invisible to everyone except her.

"Where do leprechauns come from?" Fergus narrowed his gaze. "Now, that's a question you should be asking yourself, Sabrina. Then you might be thinkin' differently about your condescending attitude toward the wee folk."

"*My* condescending attitude?" Sabrina clamped her mouth shut when she realized Harvey and Val couldn't see Fergus and thought she was talking to them.

"Yeah, Sabrina," Val said petulantly. "You're attitude stinks today. Like a water hose at a bonfire. I mean, what happened to your sense of fun?"

"It was netted, cursed, and magnetized into temporary retirement." Surrendering to Val's crestfallen expression, Sabrina quickly regrouped. It wasn't fair to spoil the holiday for Val and Harvey just because she was the target of an insulted leprechaun's revenge. "Sorry. Uh, I didn't sleep very well last night."

"That's okay," Harvey said with his adorable puppy-dog smile. "You can sleep through first period. I always do."

"So, Sabrina—are you after goin' for the king's gold, then?" Fergus asked.

"I haven't decided yet." Sabrina quickly looked up from the two-foot-tall man and smiled lamely.

"I don't decide." Harvey shrugged. "I just doze off."

"Then I'll be on me way. For now, that is." Chuckling, Fergus popped out, leaving a trail of golden dust behind him.

"Bad dreams, Sabrina?" Val asked.

"Not as bad as the approaching nightmare." Spotting Libby, Cee Cee, and Jill coming toward them, Sabrina started walking. Flanked by Harvey and Val, she had to stop when the three cheerleaders blocked the hall. They were all wearing their green and white cheerleading uniforms with green kneesocks and shamrock pins.

"Well, even the freaks are wearing the green today." Libby smiled at Harvey. "And the football team is, too. I'll save you a seat on the float, Harvey."

"Float? I wasn't aware that the school was sinking." Sabrina scowled.

"As in St. Patrick's Day parade?" Jill tossed her blond hair and smirked. "The cheerleaders and the football team are riding on the Westbridge High float."

"You are?" Val's face lit up. "I've always wanted to be in a St. Pat's parade. What if I came along as the team mascot?"

"The Westbridge mascot is a Scallion," Libby said, giving Val's all green outfit a quick once-over. "Not a cucumber."

"Oh." Val blinked, then asked hopefully, "What if I change into a white T-shirt? Then I'd look like a Scallion."

"Not a chance. I'll kiss a leprechaun and dance a jig on a toadstool before you hitch a ride with the cheerleaders." Laughing, Libby moved on. Jill and Cee Cee pushed past Sabrina to catch up.

"So much for Irish luck." Val sighed as she continued down the hall with Sabrina and Harvey. "Why doesn't Libby like me?"

"Beats me," Sabrina said honestly. "You offer yourself up as a verbal sacrifice every chance you get."

At her locker Sabrina turned the combination lock and spoke without looking at Harvey. "How come you didn't tell me you were going to be in the parade, Harvey?"

"Because I'm still hoping to get out of it." Harvey shrugged. "Being in a parade isn't exactly the most exciting way to spend St. Patrick's Day afternoon, you know?"

"Yeah, you're right," Val said. "There are a lot of better things to do than crawling down Main Street at two miles an hour behind a marching band and waving at an adoring crowd. Although, at the moment I can't think of any."

Sabrina dropped her heavy backpack on the floor as she started to open the locker door.

"Ouch!"

Sabrina flinched. *Salem?*

"Your backpack is talking," Val said evenly.

Sabrina looked up sharply. "No, it's not."

"Yes, it is." Harvey nodded. "It said 'ouch.'"

"No, it didn't." When Val and Harvey looked at each other, Sabrina pointed the cat out of the backpack and into her locker. Then she picked up the backpack and opened it. "See? Just books and notebooks."

The period warning bell rang.

"Oops!" Harvey suddenly looked frantic. "I have to drop a late book off at the library on my way to class or the parade won't be a problem. I'll be in detention. Later, Sabrina!"

"Sure!" Sabrina's eyes widened when her locker door rattled. However, Val was also in a hurry and didn't notice.

"I've gotta run, too! See you second period!" Val waved and ran toward the stairs past Mr. Kraft, who ignored the inexcusable fact that she was breaking the hall speed limit.

Sabrina sagged against her locker, hoping the vice-principal would walk on by without noticing her, either. The locker door rattled against her back.

"Let me out!"

"Quiet!" Sabrina hissed, then smiled innocently when Mr. Kraft stopped abruptly and slowly turned to regard her. "Happy St. Patrick's Day, Mr. Kraft."

"Don't push me, Sabrina!" Scowling, Mr. Kraft glanced past her. "What's making all that noise in your locker?"

Sabrina shrugged. "Could be a cat. Could be a leprechaun!"

"That's two!" Pointing a warning finger at her, the vice-principal stormed off down the hall.

Sabrina turned and yanked open the locker door. Salem stared back at her.

"What are you doing here, Salem?"

"I just wanted to get out and about for St. Patrick's Day again," Salem said dryly. "Thanks to Fergus and Hilda's escalating quarrel, I've had to huddle in a closet since I became Hilda and Zelda's family pet thirty years ago. But being stuffed in a small metal cabinet is not what I had in mind!"

"You didn't have to stow away with me to get

out and about!" Sabrina smiled inanely at two students walking by. *Great! By lunch, everyone in school will know I've been talking to my locker!*

"And I thought I might talk you into nabbing the king's gold," Salem added.

"No way!" As Sabrina raised her finger to send Salem home, Fergus popped into the locker. The cat cringed, but the leprechaun's attention was focused on Sabrina.

"So that's what it's going to be, then?" Fergus cocked his head. "Pot-luck mischief instead of a pot o' gold?"

"Is there a mall in Faery Hill?" Sabrina asked.

"Absolutely not!" Fergus huffed. "The wee craftsmen have shops!"

"Well, since I couldn't possibly do eternity without a mall, I'll just have to pass on the king's gold. Sorry." Sabrina shrugged.

"It's you who'll be sorry, I'm thinkin'." Fergus frowned.

The first-period bell rang.

"Great. Now I'm late for class."

"Better hurry," Salem said.

"Not until I send you home where you belong, Salem." Sabrina raised her finger again.

Fergus waved his hand.

A swirl of golden dust zipped around Salem and the cat vanished.

"What'd you do, Fergus?"

"Not much," Fergus said. "I just put a leprechaun charm on him for the day. Salem can

44

become invisible whenever he wants." Fergus smiled smugly. "Until midnight."

"That is so cool!" Salem's voice exclaimed.

Sabrina looked down as the cat became visible on the floor by her feet. She strongly suspected the rest of the day was going to go downhill *fast*.

Chapter 5

☆

Zelda paused at the counter in the school office. The secretary, Mrs. Atherton, was filing and had her back turned. "Excuse me. Is Mr. Kraft in?"

"Yes, but he doesn't want to be disturbed." Mrs. Atherton looked over her shoulder. "And considering the mood he's in today, I hope he stays locked in his office until the final bell."

"That bad, huh?" Zelda wondered if the vice-principal's worse-than-usual temper was related to the favor Hilda had refused to do.

"All I said was *'Erin go bragh!'* when he came in this morning." Mrs. Atherton cast a scathing glance at Mr. Kraft's door. "That is *not* a firing offense!"

"I might be able to help," Zelda offered.

"Enter at your own risk." Shaking her head, Mrs. Atherton went back to her filing.

Bracing herself, Zelda knocked on the door.

"Go away! Scram! Vamoose!" Mr. Kraft barked.

"Hilda sent me." Zelda leaned closer to the door, waiting for a response. She lost her balance and almost fell when the door flew open.

"Is she going to do it?" Looking totally frantic, Mr. Kraft wrung his hands. His hair was tousled and his glasses were slightly askew.

"Maybe we should talk inside," Zelda suggested. "In private."

"She's not going to do it." Rubbing his forehead, Mr. Kraft shuffled back across the room. "I'm doomed."

"Not necessarily." Zelda closed the door and sat in the chair in front of the desk. "Maybe someone else can help. Like me, perhaps."

Mr. Kraft fixed Zelda with a desperate gaze. "Do you sing harmony? Play the guitar? The harmonica? Bones? Bodhran?"

Zelda shook her head. "What's a bodhran?"

"An Irish drum." Pacing behind the desk, the vice-principal shook his head. "I am *definitely* doomed."

"To what?"

"Being the laughingstock of Westbridge by midnight. Maybe sooner!" Sighing, Mr. Kraft fell into his chair. "It's my own fault. But how could I refuse the perfect opportunity to realize a lifelong dream?"

"I'm lost." Resting the cookie plate on her lap,

Zelda leaned forward and put on her most charming, sympathetic face. "Run that by me again. From the top."

"Promise you won't laugh?" When Zelda nodded, Mr. Kraft took a deep breath and confessed. "I'm a folksinger. A Celtic folksinger to be precise. At least, I am at home. Where no one can *hear* me sing or play the guitar."

Zelda didn't laugh, but it wasn't easy. Afraid to say anything lest she lose control of the giggles bubbling up in her throat, she just nodded solemnly.

Bolstered by Zelda's silent acceptance, Mr. Kraft continued. "I've always wanted to be on stage, but I just never had the nerve to try. Not until I stopped by the Coffee Mug the other day and overheard the owner complaining because all the professional Irish musicians in the area were already booked for St. Patrick's Day."

"So you volunteered to play?" Zelda asked.

"It just popped out!" Mr. Kraft threw up his hands. "How did I know Mr. MacIntyre would take me up on it? He's got fliers in the window, and he's even going to pay me! It's only twenty-five bucks and tips, but—"

"That's great!" Zelda grinned with genuine enthusiasm. Although the thought of the stiff and cranky Willard Kraft crooning Irish ballads and strumming a guitar was a bit hard to imagine, it was nice to know he had a passion for something besides Hilda and tyrannical control over the local teens. "So what's the problem?"

"Stage fright!" Mr. Kraft jumped up in a panic. "I'm going to freeze! I just know it. That's why I asked Hilda to sit in with me and make it a duo."

"Oh, boy." Zelda sighed. No wonder Mr. Kraft had snarled at Mrs. Atherton. Everything Irish reminded him of his predicament. "Hilda doesn't even *listen* to Irish music, let alone play it."

"So she said." Running his hands through his hair, Mr. Kraft looked at Zelda imploringly. "Maybe you could get her to change her mind?"

"Uh—I'll try." Zelda smiled tightly. She'd rather kiss the Blarney stone, which was no easy feat. The stone was believed to endow anyone who kissed it with the gift of gab. But traditionally, in order to acquire a talent for snappy patter, kissers had to ascend to the top of a ruined castle, lie down on their backs across a deep hole, and hang on for dear life as they bent their heads back and kissed it upside down. She had almost fallen.

"But just in case she doesn't change her mind," Zelda added, "maybe you should have a backup plan."

"Right! I'll just cancel!" Mr. Kraft reached for the phone.

"And miss your only chance to make your dream come true?" Zelda asked sternly.

"Sounds a lot better than standing mute and humiliated in front of a jeering mob of disappointed Irish music lovers who are pumped up on caffeine."

"Look." Zelda firmly pressed the point. "All entertainers have the jitters before a performance. You just need a few friends in the audience to put you at ease until you get warmed up."

"I don't *have* any friends," Mr. Kraft muttered. "I've *never* had any friends."

Surprise, surprise . . . Reaching her doom-and-gloom saturation point, Zelda stood up to leave. She grabbed the cookie plate before it slid off her lap and held it out. "Hilda sent these for you."

"She did?" Mr. Kraft took the plate, noticed the icing shamrocks, and dropped it on the desk. "Thanks."

Zelda paused at the door. "Is 'Finnegan's Wake' in your repertoire?"

"Oh, absolutely. It's one of my favorite songs."

Sabrina slid into her seat in second-period history and closed her eyes. She jumped up with a gasp when someone tapped on her shoulder. "Val! Don't do that!"

"Sorry!" Val stepped back. "I didn't mean to scare you. I just thought you might want go watch the parade with me this afternoon. Since I can't be in it. If you don't have other plans. I totally understand if you have something else you want to do with someone else—"

"I'll think about it, okay? I've got a little problem I have to get rid of first." Called *Fergus!*

Sabrina sank back into her seat with a weary sigh. If she didn't find a way to counter the leprechaun's practical jokes, she was a hazard to everyone who came within ten feet of her.

"Bummer. Anything I can do to help?"

Sabrina raised an eyebrow. "Are you up for a trip over the rainbow to steal a pot of gold that could mean a life sentence of servitude to the leprechaun king if we get caught?"

"Sure!" Val laughed. "I don't know what the problem is, but at least you haven't lost your sense of humor."

"Actually, I did. Right after I lost my balance and fell into Gordie last period. He fell into Jill, who fell into—oh, never mind. Let's just say the domino effect was met with less than amused tolerance by everyone involved."

"You are such a kidder!" Still laughing, Val went to her seat in the back of the room as the bell rang.

Sabrina sagged. She wasn't kidding. In addition to orchestrating Westbridge students falling down, Fergus had kept flipping the pages of her math book, making it impossible for her to complete the assigned computations in class. Her pencil tips had all broken, and her magic wouldn't negate the leprechaun's powers so she could point them sharp again. After her third trip to the classroom pencil sharpener, she had used a pen, which had immediately run out of ink. And her calculator had come up with sixty-four as an answer regardless of what figures she entered. At this rate, she'd be having a nervous breakdown before lunch. Going after the king's gold was quickly becoming a more appealing prospect.

"So this is where you hang out all day, huh?" Salem asked.

Maybe sooner! Sabrina jumped again. It sounded like the cat was sitting on the stack of books in front of her, but since he was invisible, his location was difficult to pinpoint.

"Shhhh!" Sabrina quickly looked from side to side.

"I didn't say anything." Dan Seaver, the boy in the chair beside Sabrina, frowned. His eyes widened when a paper on his desk suddenly crumpled up into a ball and flew across the room. "Hey! That's my homework!"

Fergus again!

"Aha! Suddenly things are looking up!" Sabrina's books shifted as the invisible cat leaped off the stack to chase the paper.

"Cats are so predictable." Fergus appeared in the aisle. He rocked back on his heels and laughed as Dan chased the paper, which seemed to roll, bounce, and fly around the room of its own accord.

Ignoring Mr. Warner, who banged on his desk and shouted for order, the rest of the class erupted in laughter and hoots of encouragement.

"And have you had a change of heart about stealing the king's gold, yet?" Fergus asked.

"No." As Sabrina pulled out her red spiral notebook, Fergus calmly pushed her other books off the desk. All heads turned toward her.

"Got it!" Dan jumped to his feet, triumphantly holding up his rumpled homework paper.

"Are you quite done flinging things around the room, Ms. Spellman?" The history teacher scowled darkly.

Sabrina blinked and started to protest.

"Now, that was fun!" The invisible Salem jumped into Sabrina's lap as a student messenger entered the room.

"I trust you won't have nearly as much *fun* serving detention this afternoon, Ms. Spellman." Mr. Warner took a folded note from the messenger and opened it.

Sabrina glared at Fergus.

"Don't be lookin' at me! It's not my fault some people can't take a joke." The leprechaun rolled his eyes.

"Sabrina can't do detention today!" Val stood up. "We've got a parade!"

"Yes, you do, Ms. Birckhead." Mr. Warner waved the note. "You and Ms. Spellman are going to march right down to Mr. Kraft's office. He wants to see both of you. Immediately."

Sabrina started. She hadn't seen Mr. Kraft since before first period, so how could she have gotten a third strike against her? She still didn't know what she had done to get the first two!

"Summoned to the vice-principal's office,

huh?" Salem's invisible swishing tail brushed Sabrina's nose. "That might be good for a chuckle or two, Fergus."

"Does it bode ill for the impudent young miss?"

"Does sour milk turn a cat's stomach?" Salem asked.

"Aye, then I'm with you, Salem, me lad. I wouldn't be missin' a chance to make things worse for the disrespectful herself."

"I can't believe you're siding with Fergus against me, Salem!" Sabrina whined in a whisper.

"I can't help it, Sabrina. I live with three women! I didn't even know I *had* male bonding issues."

The leprechaun grinned, then vanished as Salem leaped off Sabrina's lap.

"Why me?" Val picked up her books and trudged toward the door, muttering as Sabrina caught up. "Do you get cool points for being called into Mr. Kraft's office? 'Cause if it's cool, I don't mind. Even though I'm sure I didn't do anything."

"Neither did I." Sabrina shrugged. "Unless I broke some unwritten code of student-vice-principal conduct because I was *nice* to Mr. Kraft this morning."

"Gee. That always works for Libby."

Libby, however, was already in Mr. Kraft's office. Her face paled and her hand shot out in a stopping motion when she saw them enter. "Wait a minute!"

Sabrina and Val halted just inside the door, then stumbled forward when Harvey ran into them.

"I thought you wanted to see *me* about something important, Mr. Kraft!" Libby's dark eyes flashed indignantly. "What's with the Gaelic geek squad?"

"That's how desperate I am!" Mr. Kraft eyed the bewildered trio in the doorway with a grimace. "I really am doomed."

The invisible Salem rubbed against Sabrina's leg. Fergus appeared on a shelf behind Mr. Kraft's desk. He stretched out, propped his head on one hand, and waved at Sabrina with the other.

"I suppose you're all wondering why I asked you here." The vice-principal perched on the edge of his desk.

"I certainly am." Crossing her arms, Libby scowled. "Since I have absolutely nothing in common with *them.*"

"Asked?" Harvey blinked. "You mean we had a choice?"

"Not really." Mr. Kraft removed his glasses and rubbed his eyes. "But you all do have one thing in common."

"Beyond our mutual loathing?" Sabrina looked at Libby.

"Are we in trouble?" Val's voice cracked slightly. "Because if we aren't, I'd like to know before I fall on my knees and start begging for mercy."

"No, you're not in trouble." Replacing his glasses, Mr. Kraft took a deep breath.

"That's a relief." Harvey relaxed. "I thought for sure putting green food coloring in the soap dispensers—"

Sabrina elbowed Harvey in the ribs to silence him. Once again Mr. Kraft surprised her by ignoring a chance to add another notch to his detention slip pad.

"The school band contest proved that you all have a degree of musical talent," Mr. Kraft said. "Extremely *varied* degrees, I admit, but there's no one else I can turn to. No one I can *order* to help me out anyway."

"Help with what, Mr. Kraft?" Libby sat down and gave the despondent man her undivided attention. Hooked on power and status, she never missed an advancement opportunity.

Sabrina wilted as she took a seat along the back wall with Harvey and Val. The musical ability they had demonstrated in the battle of the bands had come from a bottle of magically produced talent. She had dispensed an antidote when fame had threatened their friendship. Now the plumbing once again seized up whenever she sang in the shower.

No one said a word while Mr. Kraft explained that he was making his musical debut at a local coffeehouse that evening and wanted them to attend for moral support. When he finished, they all stared at him in mute shock for several prolonged seconds.

"So. Now that that's settled—" Smiling tightly, Mr. Kraft picked up a stack of papers.

"What's settled?" Libby jumped to her feet. "I don't mind helping you warm up an audience, Mr. Kraft, but I'm *not* sitting at a table in a public place with those—those socially and musically challenged Irish wannabes!"

Mr. Kraft's face twisted into a pained expression. "Pleeease!"

"What?" Salem sat up in Sabrina's lap. "This isn't the hard-nosed, despicable Willard Kraft I've come to know and ridicule."

"Watch what you say, Sabrina!" Val hissed into her ear. "And when did you turn into a baritone?"

Sabrina quickly covered the invisible cat's outburst and his mouth. "My vocal chords constrict when I'm totally astonished. Which doesn't happen much anymore."

"Willard seems a bit of a wimp to me." Fergus disappeared from the bookshelf, then reappeared on the desk and stared unseen into Mr. Kraft's face. "But he does have impressively beady eyes, a sure sign of a stubborn, ill-tempered cad. I like him."

"That figures," Sabrina muttered.

Libby cocked an eyebrow at Mr. Kraft, then

shrugged. "I suppose having the vice-principal plead is worth something. But the potential damage to my dignity requires a little more incentive."

"How about a limo to take the cheerleading squad to away games?" Mr. Kraft held his breath.

Libby extended her hand. "Deal."

"Excellent." Exhaling, Mr. Kraft began handing out the sheets of paper. "These are the lyrics to the choruses—"

"Hold it!" Sabrina stood up, dumping Salem off her lap.

"Thanks for the warning!" Salem said. "Even garbage trucks *beep* when they're gonna back up!"

Mr. Kraft's eyes widened. "The baritone is a nice touch, Sabrina, but what do garbage trucks have to do with my gig?"

"Nothing. I just want to know what Harvey and Val and I are going to get out of it." Sabrina faltered when Mr. Kraft's gaze narrowed again. "Not that we wouldn't be glad to help, but Libby *is* getting your eternal gratitude and a limo—"

"Libby can sing." Mr. Kraft smiled. "And *you* won't get suspended on a trumped-up charge."

"That sounds fair." Sabrina nodded, then glanced at Harvey and Val. "Doesn't that sound fair?"

"No," Harvey said, "but nobody ever said vice-principals were fair."

"I'm in!" Grinning, Val raised her hand.

"Great." After Mr. Kraft finished handing out

the lyric sheets, he picked up the cookie plate he had dropped on the desk earlier. "Have a cookie."

"How sweet, Mr. Kraft!" Libby helped herself and took a dainty bite. "Oh, these are delicious."

"They are, aren't they?" Val nodded as she chewed.

"These look just like Aunt Hilda's shamrock cookies." Sabrina took a bite. "Except these taste a little funny."

"How funny?" Salem asked.

"They *are* your aunt Hilda's cookies," Mr. Kraft said. "Zelda dropped them off a little while ago."

"Where'd that black cat come from?" Harvey rubbed his eyes.

"What black cat?" Mr. Kraft swallowed, then froze as he reached for another cookie. "There's a little man standing on my desk."

Val giggled, then gasped. "Ohmigosh! It's a real live leprechaun!"

"Aye and I am that." Fergus whipped his hat off his head and bowed. "Fergus, at your service."

"Cool! I'm Harvey."

"There's no such thing as leprechauns!" Libby scowled.

Sabrina just stared.

"How come I'm not invisible anymore?" Salem whined.

No one, Sabrina noticed, seemed upset by the amazing presence of a leprechaun and a talking cat.

"And would you not be believin' your own eyes, then, lass?" Fergus glanced at Libby as he flipped his hat back onto his head.

As usual, the cheerleader was not intimidated. "I see a scruffy-looking old guy with a severe growth deficiency."

Recovering, Sabrina glared at Fergus. "You switched the cookie plates! Aunt Hilda wouldn't have deliberately sent the *real* shamrock cookies to Mr. Kraft."

"Aye and I did."

"Don't I get three wishes or something?" Mr. Kraft asked. He was remarkably calm under the circumstances.

"Only if you catch one of the wee folk, which you didn't. However, would you be interested in findin' the pot of gold at the end of the rainbow?" A cloud of golden dust swirled through the room as Fergus waved his hand.

The mortals gasped in awe as the end of a glorious rainbow suddenly filled the far side of the room.

Sabrina groaned.

Chapter 6

☆

☆

Hilda trudged in the kitchen door, dropped her violin case on the table, and sank into a chair. With a quick apathetic point, she changed out of her green suit into green leggings and a bulky cream-colored sweater with a shamrock appliqué.

Zelda lowered her newspaper and frowned. "What went wrong?"

"Nothing." Hilda shrugged. "I played well, but so did everyone else who showed up for the audition."

"Then you've got a chance, right?"

"I suppose. After listening to twenty other virtuosos perform perfectly, I got nervous and warmed up with a few bars of 'The Tangled-Finger Tango.'" Hilda shuddered. "I almost froze!"

"Really?" Nodding, Zelda pointed to refill her cup of herbal tea, then zapped up a cup of Hilda's favorite brew. "It's not like you to get stage fright."

"Especially after a couple hundred years of auditions blown and better forgotten." Hilda sipped her tea and sighed again. "I've developed a thick skin over the decades, but twenty pairs of critical eyes could strip the hide off an alligator. As it was, my worthy competition put some definitive dents in my professional aplomb."

"Which makes me wonder why you refused to help Mr. Kraft out at his coffeehouse gig tonight." The newspaper vanished with a quick point, and Zelda folded her arms on the table. "Your intense revulsion to Irish music aside."

"He told you?"

Zelda nodded. "He's more panic stricken than the students he calls into his office."

"That bad, huh?" Hilda reached for a cookie.

Zelda stayed her hand. "Those are the real shamrock cookies, Hilda!"

"I get hungry under pressure. And coping with a few faeries raiding the spell ingredient cabinet might take my mind off the audition." Hilda chomped, chewed, and swallowed. "And Willard."

"Well, I've already decided to go to the Coffee Mug tonight to give him some moral support. And I think you should sit in and help him out. Even if he is the worst date you've ever had."

"Not quite the worst, but close." Hilda grimaced. "Going to dinner with a six-year-old version of Willard wasn't a picnic, but at least he never stands on tavern tables testing political slogans on the customers like Patrick Henry."

"'Give me liberty or give me death!' was a keeper, though."

"Much better than his first version. I don't think history would have immortalized 'Freedom or I'm out of here!'" Hilda glanced around the kitchen and frowned.

"What?" Zelda followed Hilda's bewildered gaze. "Did I forget to take the decorative chains and manacles back to the dungeon after I polished them?"

"I don't see any faeries," Hilda said. "No leprechauns or pixies, either. Strange."

"Maybe none of the mischievous, thieving"— Zelda hesitated, amending her statement just in case she was overheard—"but *charming* little people are here."

"When was the last time we didn't 'lose' trinkets, jewelry, or snacks to a light-fingered wee person on St. Patrick's Day?" Hilda looked up and around. "Not that we mind, of course."

"Never. Not that I recall." Zelda peeked under the table. "Oh, my."

"What?" Hilda bent over just in time to see a gaudy rhinestone earring, a premeasured packet of toodle-loo-and-good-riddance powder, and a small salt shaker fall on the floor, as though they had just been dropped from invisible hands. If she had just eaten a real shamrock cookie, she'd be able to see the tiny being responsible.

Hilda and Zelda both sat bolt upright. They glanced at the cookie plate, then at each other.

"Fergus must have switched the plates!" Zelda fumed. "When he dusted that golden dust off his jacket."

"But if these aren't the real shamrock cookies, then—" Hilda paled.

"I gave the real shamrock cookies to Mr. Kraft," Zelda finished.

"Willard can't do little people! Especially leprechauns. By comparison, normal teenagers are polite, respectful prudes. He'll go completely mad!"

"Maybe it's not too late. He didn't seem terribly thrilled with the cookies when I delivered them." Zelda raised her finger. "Let's go."

"Please, don't take my fiddle!" Hilda begged the unseen wee folk as she popped out. "Or my mace!"

Before Sabrina realized what Mr. Kraft was up to, the vice-principal cracked open his office door and handed Mrs. Atherton the plate of real shamrock cookies. Apparently, he didn't realize or didn't care that the cookies had made it possible for him and the others to see Fergus and the amazing rainbow.

"Sorry I snapped at you earlier, Mrs. Atherton."

Stunned, the secretary took the cookie peace offering and smiled. "Thank you, Mr. Kraft."

"But—" Sabrina started to protest, but Mr. Kraft silenced her with a warning glance as he returned to the chair behind his desk.

"Looks as if we're not the only ones who are going to have an interesting St. Patrick's Day," Salem said.

"Okay, Fergus. Let me get this straight." Mr. Kraft steepled his fingers and warily eyed the little man lounging on the desk in front of him. "If we take a ride on that rainbow, we'll find a pot of gold at the end of the line."

"Yes, and that's the truth of it." Fergus nodded. "An even split for all."

"Mr. Kraft—" Trying to be patient, Sabrina leaned forward. "If King Kevin catches you, you'll be a prisoner in Faery Hill forever. Do you really want to do forever with a bunch of tiny guys who don't know the meaning of the word *discipline?*"

"I'd rather be rich. And if I'm rich, I'll never have to talk to another teenager again." Mr. Kraft smiled. "I'm going."

"Well, if Mr. Kraft's going, I'm going, too." Libby cocked her head thoughtfully. "Gold is going up on the stock market again. I could shop till I drop on the interest!"

"That's a lot of sushi, all right," Salem agreed.

"I wouldn't miss it!" Val bubbled with enthusiasm. "I mean, think of it! Leprechauns and pots of gold and rainbows! What an awesome way to spend St. Patrick's Day!"

"Sounds more exciting than riding in the Westbridge parade," Harvey said.

Sabrina threw up her hands. Contrary to Aunt Hilda's prediction, her mortal friends and the vice-principal had not freaked out when confronted with a sarcastically verbal cat and a leprechaun. Their calm acceptance of Fergus and his proposal was worse, though.

"I'm ready whenever you are." Mr. Kraft stood up and straightened his glasses.

"Excellent." Grinning, Fergus leaped off the desk and swept his arm toward the rainbow. A door opened in the kaleidoscope mist, revealing a rainbow-colored escalator. "This way, if you please."

Sabrina dropped her forehead in her hand as Mr. Kraft, Libby, Val, Harvey, and Salem trooped by her. Even though she had only been coping with Fergus for a few hours, she was sure there was a catch to this deal, too. She rose and walked to the end of the line forming by the open door.

"Oh, great! You decided to come, Sabrina." Val's eyes were bright with anticipation.

"I can't very well let my best friends and my two worst enemies ride the Fairy Land Express to certain catastrophe without me." *Can I?*

"But does he have to come?" Mr. Kraft looked down at the black cat sitting behind him. "The only thing worse than an impudent kid is a smart-alecky cat."

"That remains to be seen." Sabrina scowled at Fergus.

"Guess I'm elected to go first." Rubbing his hands on his jeans, Harvey entered the door and turned right to mount the escalator. The instant he moved onto the first step, the moving stairs stopped.

"Just move up a few steps, Harvey, me lad. It'll start again as soon as we're all aboard," Fergus explained. "And please be holdin' on to those overhead straps. I wouldn't want to be flinging anyone off into the untamed spectrum before we get where we're goin'."

"What happens in the untamed spectrum?" Libby asked.

"'Tis a terrible fate you'd be knowin' for sure," Fergus said. "When you finally find your way out, you'll have no sense of color left a'tall."

"A color-coordination disorder?" Appalled, Libby tightened her grip on the strap above her. "Why didn't you warn me before?"

"Disclosure isn't high on his list of priorities," Sabrina said.

"I'd rather flunk chemistry than clash!"

One by one the Westbridge High rainbow riders mounted the stairs. Bringing up the rear, Sabrina stepped in, picked up Salem, then reached for the strap. Her fingers had barely closed around it before the escalator took off.

"Whooooaaaaaa!" Harvey yelled as the moving staircase accelerated to high speed in nothing flat, then whisked them into a crayon-box version of a jump to light-speed.

Eyes wide with terror, Mr. Kraft clutched his strap with both hands. Libby screamed and Val closed her eyes. Salem dug into Sabrina's thin shirt with his claws. Hanging on to the cat with one hand and the strap with the other, Sabrina winced as streams of variegated color whizzed by.

When the rainbow escalator ride suddenly slowed and stopped, they were all breathless with fear and exhilaration.

"I think I'm going to faint," Val gasped.

"Man! That was better than the Maniac Looper at Watkins Park!" Grinning, Harvey glanced back over his shoulder and frowned. "I think Mr. Kraft stopped breathing."

"Panic does that to a person," Fergus said. He smiled when the vice-principal exhaled loudly, releasing all the air he had been holding in his lungs. Libby took Mr. Kraft's arm to steady him as the rainbow door slid open.

Last on, first off, Sabrina stumbled out the door into a lush green clearing in a thick forest of huge trees. Brightly colored wildflowers waved in a slight breeze.

"This doesn't look right." Jumping out of Sabrina's arms, Salem sniffed the air.

"Oh, this is beautiful!" Instantly recovering from their mad dash across rainbow hyperspace, Val looked around in wide-eyed wonder. "Where are we?"

"Ireland." Fergus beamed.

Mr. Kraft scowled and his voice cracked slightly when he spoke. "But these trees look like they're hundreds of years old. Primal growth. I thought most of the Emerald Isle forests had been cut down during the last few centuries."

Fergus nodded. "Aye and they were."

"What's that?" Libby squealed and ducked behind the vice-principal as an animal the size of a bull moose with pointed antlers walked into the clearing.

"An Irish elk," Fergus said with a sad smile. "A sight none will be seein' in the twenty-first century. They've been extinct for a thousand years."

Sabrina stared in awe as the giant elk paused with its majestic head held high. It bolted back into the forest when it caught their scent. Her brain clicked back into gear just as suddenly. "Wait a minute! I know where we are, Fergus, but when are we?"

"I don't know, but the dress code could use some work." Libby sneered as several men with long, flowing hair emerged from behind several trees on the far side of the open meadow. They all wore coarse, belted tunics, sandals or boots, and carried leather shields, swords, and spears.

"When? Oh, roughly nineteen hundred B.C."

Fergus smirked as he pointed toward the tall, striking man who was obviously the leader of the barbarian band. "That's Lugh of the long arm. One of me most famous and revered ancestors."

Libby gave Fergus a quick once-over. "The tall gene must be recessive."

"Funny. He doesn't look like a 'Lou,'" Harvey said. "He looks mad."

"Maybe they're from the Welcome Wagon?" Val suggested hopefully.

"Looks to me as if it's time to circle the wagons." Salem took cover behind Sabrina. "If we had wagons—"

Mr. Kraft flinched as the fierce-looking Lugh slowly advanced across the clearing. Then the vice-principal clapped his hands together as though to hurry things up during a school fire drill. "Okay, people! Let's go! We're getting out of here now!"

"Well, now, here's the thing of it." Fergus blocked Mr. Kraft as the vice-principal turned to go back to the rainbow. "You can't be leavin' just yet."

"I knew it!" Sabrina glared at the leprechaun. "What's the catch this time?"

"It's just that you can't be goin' home until you reach the end of the rainbow. And you can't be takin' the rainbow any farther unless he grants you passage." Fergus waved toward Lugh as the warrior raised his arm and quickened his pace.

"I know that look," Sabrina said, her gaze

fastened on Lugh's ferocious face. "That's how you look, Mr. Kraft. Right before you storm the cafeteria to stop a food fight."

"In that case—" Mr. Kraft folded his glasses and slipped them into his shirt pocket. "Run!"

They ran—with Lugh and his men charging after them, screeching like a band of tone-deaf banshees.

Chapter 7

Hilda and Zelda walked briskly into the empty school office and headed straight for Mr. Kraft's inner sanctum. No one tried to stop them.

Bursting through the door, Zelda stopped abruptly. "Uh-oh. We're too late."

"How do you know?" Hilda stopped behind Zelda just as the rainbow in the corner faded from sight. "Oh, boy."

"'Oh, Fergus' might be more accurate." Shaking her head, Zelda slumped against the doorjamb. "Poor Mr. Kraft."

"Come on!" Hilda laughed shortly. "Do you honestly think Willard could be conned into going after a pot of gold at the end of the rainbow by a leprechaun? He doesn't have a fanciful bone in his old, stodgy body!"

"How long has Fergus been trying to get you to go after King Kevin's gold?" Zelda asked.

"As long as I've known the little hustler," Hilda said. "Like I don't have anything better to do than take the Rambo rainbow ride to an eternity of spit-polishing shoes for King Kevin."

"I doubt that Fergus told Mr. Kraft the downside." Zelda shrugged. "Then again, who knows? Maybe the idea appealed to Mr. Kraft's spirit of adventure."

Hilda raised a skeptical eyebrow. "Willard's idea of pushing the risk envelope is nudging the speedometer two miles over the speed limit."

"W-w-who's there?" Mrs. Atherton's voice squeaked.

Hilda looked back to see the school secretary standing in the open doorway. The shaken woman was gripping a stapler to her chest, and her wide eyes looked dazed.

"It's just us, Mrs. Atherton," Zelda said. "Hilda and Zelda Spellman."

"Oh, I thought they were in here." Mrs. Atherton started to relax, then wildly scanned the interior of the office. "Where's Mr. Kraft? And Sabrina and the others?"

"Sabrina and what others?" Hilda tensed.

"Harvey Kinkle and Val Birckhead and Libby Chessler! They were all in here a few minutes ago. I would have heard them leave—even though I was cowering behind the counter."

Hilda wilted. If Mr. Kraft, Sabrina, and her

friends had all boarded the rainbow, there was nothing she or Zelda could do to help them. They were off to Tir na nOg, the mythical Celtic land of the ever young and all time, beyond the reach of Other Realm magic, trapped in the capricious meanderings of the rainbow transit until they reached the end of the line.

If they reached the end of the line.

Where King Kevin would snare them the instant anyone touched his precious pot of gold.

"I'm sure they'll be all right," Zelda said with more conviction than she probably felt.

"At least, Sabrina's magic will work." Hilda sighed. "Won't it?"

"There's another one!" Mrs. Atherton shrieked and waved her arms. "Shoo! Shoo!"

Zelda's gaze snapped to Mr. Kraft's desk. "The cookies are gone!"

"Oops!" Hilda turned to see Mrs. Atherton tugging on the stapler, which an invisible wee person was obviously trying to pull out of her grasp. "So much for our tranquil St. Patrick's Day."

"Give that back!" Mrs. Atherton snapped. "Let go!"

"It's just a stapler, Mrs. Atherton," Zelda said gently. "Let the leprechaun have it. It'll take weeks to put Mr. Kraft's office back together if the leprechaun throws a temper tantrum."

Mrs. Atherton let go, and one end of the stapler

fell to the floor. The chubby leprechaun culprit appeared just long enough to smile and thank Zelda.

"Any time you'd be needin' a favor, just give Patrick O'Flannigan a call." With a wink, Patrick and the stapler disappeared.

"I think it would be safer to invite myself to dinner with a shark," Zelda said.

Collecting herself, Mrs. Atherton smoothed her hair back and breathed in deeply. "Did a leprechaun just steal my stapler?"

"Yes. It's sort of a St. Patrick's Day tradition among the little people to plunder and pilfer the mortal realm," Hilda said truthfully. She knew that once the effects of the shamrock wore off, Mrs. Atherton's memory would become fuzzy and fade.

"Where are the cookies I brought Mr. Kraft, Mrs. Atherton?" Zelda asked.

"Those delicious shamrock ones he gave to me? As though that would make up for his foul humor and insensitive remarks?" Mrs. Atherton scowled. "I ate one and gave the rest to Mrs. Quick."

"The math teacher?" Hilda smiled expectantly. "And where did Mrs. Quick go?"

"To the staging area for the St. Patrick's Day Parade with the cheerleaders. They have to finish the Westbridge High float, and she's the faculty adviser."

Zelda groaned. "Murphy's Law. If things can get worse, they will."

"Leave it to an Irishman to write a law that Fate never breaks." Hilda flicked her finger, installing a rainbow pager in the corner of the room. When the rainbow returned, she would be notified. Then, grabbing Zelda's arm, she dragged her toward the door. "Come on. You wanted to see the parade."

"But I didn't want to be responsible for wee folk damage control!"

As they ran from the office, Mrs. Atherton hollered behind them. "Hey! That's Mr. Kraft's favorite paperweight!" The secretary paused. "On second thought, take it! Take anything you want."

"Oh, no. Here he comes." Mr. Kraft wiped the sweat from his brow with his shirtsleeve as Lugh of the long arm strode forward.

Sabrina sighed. After being run down and rounded up, the rainbow invaders had been escorted into Lugh's camp. They had been sitting on a rough log under guard for fifteen minutes, waiting for Lugh to determine their fate. The sun was sinking low in the sky, and a curious crowd had gathered near the well a short distance away.

"He's not bad-looking for a barbarian." Libby shook out her long hair and smiled. "Maybe I can charm him into letting us go."

"That's about as likely as cobras becoming America's favorite house pet," Salem said.

Libby's eyes flashed. "At least I don't spit on myself and call it a bath, cat!"

Val wrinkled her nose. "Considering the stench, I don't think spit baths would bother Lugh."

Harvey grimaced. "Considering the stench, I don't think Lugh bothers with any kind of bath."

"Actually, I think the smell is coming from that bog over there." Mr. Kraft waved toward the marsh.

Fergus suddenly appeared on the end of the log. "Lugh's a fine, strappin' young lad, if I do say so meself. Master of the sun, art, and medicine, he is."

"And he's an ancestor of yours, Fergus?" Sabrina cocked her head and studied the approaching warrior. Tall and muscular with long hair and blue eyes, Lugh was gorgeous in spite of his primitive attire and behavior. "Sorry, but I don't see the family resemblance."

Fergus bristled. "That's because over the centuries, those with no respect for Irish culture have reduced Lugh and the mighty Tuatha de Danaan into the likes of me and my faery kin. Aye, and I'm tellin' it true."

Everyone tensed as Lugh stopped before Mr. Kraft. The vice-principal smiled tightly, then quickly raised and lowered his palm in a nervous greeting.

Lugh looked at him coldly. "You're a pitiful mite of a man, aren't you, then?"

"Yes! Absolutely." Mr. Kraft nodded.

"Ha!" Lugh threw back his head and folded his arms over his broad chest. "And a poor excuse for a spy, I'm thinkin'."

"Spy? For whom?" Sabrina asked.

"Balor of the Evil Eye!" Lugh roared. "And who else but the dark ruler's spies would be invadin' my camp on the eve of the battle between the forces of light and darkness?"

"We're not spies. Oh, no, sir." Mr. Kraft shook his head emphatically, then cleared his throat with a glance toward Fergus. "In fact, we're, uh— friends of the family! Your family!"

"Who's Balor?" Sabrina frowned.

"Do I look like a spy?" Libby tilted her head and batted her large, dark eyes.

Lugh gave the cheerleader his own version of the Chessler once-over. "You look like somethin' the cat dragged in."

"I beg your pardon." Salem's head snapped up. "Cats have better taste!"

Libby sat back, stricken.

"Huh?" Sabrina looked at Fergus.

"Lugh doesn't see you as you are, but as you would look in his time." Fergus sighed. "He can't see or hear me a'tall, more's the shame of it. I'm not allowed to interfere."

"So—when is this battle supposed to go down?" Harvey asked anxiously.

"Probably tomorrow at dawn," Val muttered, then flinched when Lugh pointed at her.

"There! And how would you be knowin' that if you weren't spyin' for Balor?"

"Uh—a lucky guess?" Val cringed under Lugh's intense and icy gaze.

"Darn!" Mr. Kraft stood up and snapped his fingers. "We left the rainbow running—"

"And bein' as you're spies"—Lugh pushed Mr. Kraft back down—"you won't be goin' anywhere."

"Sorry, Lugh, but we've got to get going, and we need your okay to do it." Sabrina stood up and raised her finger. "So what's it gonna be? Permission to pass or a dose of my powerful magic?"

"Sabrina!" Mr. Kraft snapped. "Don't make threats you can't back up! There's no such thing as magic!"

"Excuse mc, Mr. Kraft?" Sabrina rolled her eyes. "You just rode a rainbow four thousand years into the past with a leprechaun and a talking cat. I think I can manage a little magic."

"Except it won't work on Lugh," Fergus said.

Sabrina paled. "My magic won't work here?"

"Oh, no. It'll work fine. But the Tuatha de Danaan are the magic people. I seriously doubt Lugh will be impressed."

"We'll just see about that." Bracing herself, Sabrina pointed at a nearby thatched hut.

"So Mr. Kraft and Lugh have proof,
magic finger, raise that roof."

Everyone but Fergus and Lugh gawked as the roof made of bound sheaves of dried grass lifted six feet above the primitive dwelling and hovered.

"That is astonishing, Sabrina!" Mr. Kraft adjusted his glasses and squinted.

"That's nothing. Wait until I get warmed up."

Shaking his head, Lugh raised his hand. The roof settled back into place with a casual flick of his finger.

"So—" Libby turned to Fergus. "What will impress him?"

"Very little, I'm afraid." Val slumped.

"Actually, the Danaan believe that music has a spell-weaving power." Fergus tapped his cheek with his finger and nodded. "A bit of song that will inspire them to victory in the battle ahead might do it."

"A song?" Sabrina hesitated, then shrugged. Smiling, she pointed a small harp into Mr. Kraft's hands and the ability to play it into his fingers. "Okay, Mr. Kraft. You're on!"

"Me? Oh, no. I can't. I mean, I play the guitar, not the harp." Mr. Kraft almost dropped the stringed instrument as he jumped back to his feet.

"Are you a minstrel, then, or no?" Lugh asked curiously.

"He's great!" Harvey stood up and slapped Mr. Kraft on the back. "He's even got a real gig at the Coffee Mug tonight."

"Of course, it remains to be seen if he'll survive to get a second one," Salem said.

"So be it." Stepping aside, Lugh motioned Mr. Kraft into the center of the crowd gathered around the fire. "Your song will determine your fate."

"Go, Mr. Kraft!" Grinning, Val punched her fist into the air. She pulled it back when she noticed the grim expressions on the warrior faces surrounding them.

"And I thought the coffeehouse crowd was going to be a tough audience." Gripping the harp, Mr. Kraft sat on a stool someone shoved under him. Licking dry lips, he tentatively placed his fingers on the strings. A haunting, clear melody rang through the still twilight. "Hey! I can play Thomas Moore's 'The Minstrel Boy' on this thing!"

"What do you know." Harvey nudged Val. "Mr. Kraft can smile."

Sabrina made a circling motion with her hand, urging the vice-principal to get on with it. Lugh's band of not-so-merry men was getting restless.

Taking a deep breath, Mr. Kraft started to sing. "'The Minstrel Bo-oy to the—'" His voice cracked on the first few notes.

An audible rumbling stirred through the crowd. Lugh winced.

White as a sheet and trembling, Mr. Kraft paused, then plunged ahead. "'—to the war has gone, in the ranks of death you'll find him.'"

"This is supposed to inspire Lugh to victory?" Libby asked, then lapsed into pained silence.

However, once he got going, Mr. Kraft belted out the rest of the song with only a few nervous squeaks and off-key notes. He knew all the lyrics, which told of a courageous warrior boy who fought for freedom with a sword in his hand and a harp slung over his shoulder.

" 'Thy songs were made for the pure and freeeeeeeee!' " Mr. Kraft's fingers flew over the strings as he wound up for his big finish. " 'They shall never sound in slaaaa-ver-eeeee!' "

Total silence reigned for a long moment when the last chord on the harp faded. Mr. Kraft's hesitant smile waned as Lugh's unsmiling men slowly began to advance on him.

"I guess they didn't like it?" Val shifted nervously.

"Everyone's a critic," Sabrina said.

Chapter 8

Since the parade route had been cordoned off, the other Westbridge streets were jammed with traffic. The sidewalks, shops, and cafés were also packed with people celebrating the Irish holiday. When Hilda and Zelda finally got within two blocks of the parade staging area, there was no place to park.

"Why did we bring the car?" Unnerved, Zelda gripped the steering wheel in white-knuckled frustration.

"Because you're an overachiever who likes competing with mortals on their own turf even though it's inconvenient, inefficient, and insane." Hilda peered through the windshield. "Pull into that alley."

"It's a one-way street and we're going the wrong

way!" Zelda jumped when the driver behind them leaned on his horn.

"Just do it, Zelda!" As Zelda yanked the steering wheel to the left, Hilda tossed a quick point behind her and smiled smugly when the annoyed driver pounded on his suddenly silenced horn.

Zelda stopped the car in an unloading zone and glanced at the No Parking signs lining the narrow passage. "We can't park here."

"I know." Hilda got out, walked around the front of the car, and opened Zelda's door. "Come on, Zelda. The sanity of Mrs. Quick and the Westbridge High cheerleading squad is at stake."

Nodding, Zelda put the keys in her pocket and stepped out. "I've never had a parking ticket."

"And you won't get one now, either." The instant the door closed, Hilda flicked her finger and the car vanished. "There's no law against parking in your own driveway."

Zelda blinked. "I think I'd better reread Dr. Chango's *Living among Mortals: It's Okay to Have a Magic Edge.*"

Heading out of the alley on foot, Hilda and Zelda both started when a patrol car suddenly pulled up to block the entrance.

"Hold it right there, ladies." A police officer emerged from the car and flipped open a yellow citation pad.

"What's the problem, Officer?" Hilda asked innocently.

"I hardly know where to begin. Going the wrong way on a one-way street. Parking in a no-parking zone." The policeman glanced down the alley and frowned. "Where's your car?"

"What car?" Waving farewell to the baffled officer, Hilda hauled Zelda down the sidewalk toward the park two blocks away.

A crowd was already beginning to gather on the curb along the parade route. Young mothers pushed strollers decked out with green crepe paper. Old men waved green, orange, and white striped Irish flags. Everyone was dressed in some shade of green.

"I am definitely losing my edge," Zelda muttered as they skirted the throng.

"Forget it, Zelda. It's a beautiful day for a March parade, and Fergus isn't here. Let's enjoy it." Hilda walked faster as they neared the barricades across the entrance to the parking lot where the floats were assembling.

"How can you even think about having a good time?" Zelda huffed. "I certainly can't. Not with Sabrina and her friends rambling through Irish history with that devious little imp, Fergus, on a doomed mission to steal King Kevin's pot of gold."

"Is there anything we can do about it?" Hilda turned to walk around the end of the temporary barrier.

"No, but—"

"Halt!" A security guard shouted and waved at them to stop. Planting himself in their path, he planted his hands on his hips. "What d'ya think you're doing? Nobody is allowed in here unless they're participants in the parade."

"This is an emergency!" Hilda looked past the guard. The Westbridge High float was easy to spot.

Decked out in the school colors, the green and white display had three risers positioned under a football goalpost. Large green shamrocks adorned the side posts. A football was sailing over the goal, held in place by a thick wire. Mrs. Quick was inspecting the flower decorations while the cheerleaders anxiously watched. At least no one was freaking out. Either they hadn't eaten the shamrock cookies yet, or the wee folk were boycotting the Westbridge parade.

"And what emergency might that be?" The guard shifted his suspicious gaze between Hilda and Zelda. "Aside from wanting to get a better view than everyone else in Westbridge."

"We're, uh—with the band!" Zelda cast a casual point behind Hilda. "And we're late."

Hilda's head snapped around as her violin case appeared on the ground behind her.

"What band is that? The Ditsy Blond and Bungle Corps? Nice try." The guard dismissed them with an annoyed wave. "Get out of here."

"Show him, Hilda." Crossing her arms, Zelda

stood her ground. "Play a few bars of something Irish."

"You're not serious!"

Zelda leaned closer and whispered. "Play and I'll agree to get that 'Mr. Potion' machine you've been hounding me about."

From the corner of her eye, Hilda saw Mrs. Quick lift the cookie plate off the float. Running her hand through her hair, she fired off a couple quick points of her own. "Okay. I will, if you will."

Bewildered, Zelda frowned. Her eyes widened when Hilda gestured toward the round canvas bodhran case she had just zapped. "But I can't—"

"Fake it! Hold the stick like a pencil and move your hand up and down very fast." Hilda leaned over, unsnapped her case, and took out her violin. "Just try to keep the beat."

Smiling self-consciously, Zelda unzipped the bodhran case and removed a round drum that was four inches deep and eighteen inches in diameter. Holding it by the crossbar in back, she gripped the stick with bulbous ends in her left hand and tentatively struck the cowhide head. The bodhran boomed with a deep, mellow tone.

Hilda fitted her violin under her chin and winced as she began playing a lively traditional Irish jig. Although her hand only moved at half-speed, Zelda managed to keep the six-beat rhythm.

Hilda stopped playing after completing the A melody of the two-part tune and glared at the guard. "There! Satisfied?"

The ranger was obviously impressed. "You play a dandy fiddle, lady! You wouldn't happen to know—"

One of the cheerleaders screamed.

Sabrina raised her finger to pop Mr. Kraft out of harm's way as Lugh's warriors closed in. However, when the men were within a few feet of the cringing vice-principal, they suddenly burst into thunderous cheers.

"You foretell a great victory for the forces of light, minstrel." Lugh nodded in majestic approval. "Inspired by your song, we will defeat the evil Balor!"

"The neighborhood cat chorus never gets that kind of reception." Salem sighed. "Maybe we just need more practice."

"Any more practice and the neighborhood will make sure the cat chorus rehearses at the pound." Sabrina stooped over to whisper to Fergus. "Does Lugh win?"

"Of course!" Fergus beamed.

"You and your people are free to pass, minstrel." Lugh swept his arm toward the rainbow at the edge of the clearing.

With an enthusiastic display of spear shaking and more shouting, Lugh's men parted to let Mr. Kraft exit the circle.

Thrilled by the unexpected accolades, Mr. Kraft paused. "How about an encore?"

Sabrina pointed the harp out of existence. "Let's not push our luck, Mr. Kraft."

"You should always leave them asking for more," Libby added.

"Oh, right! I forgot." As the rainbow riders headed out, Mr. Kraft turned and bowed repeatedly until Harvey yanked him off his feet and urged him forward. "What are you doing, Kinkle?"

"I don't know about you, Mr. Kraft," Harvey said, "but I'd rather not be left behind and drafted into Lugh's army."

"Point taken."

Fergus waited until everyone was inside the rainbow and holding on before he boarded. "And let's be hopin' you have the same success at our next stop."

"Which is whaaahhh . . ." Val's conversational tone became a wail of startled fright as the bottom dropped out of the rainbow.

Clutching Salem and her strap, Sabrina shrieked along with everyone else as they plunged into a seemingly bottomless chasm of chaotic color.

"I don't want to be a kitty pancaaaaake!" Salem buried his head against Sabrina's shoulder.

Sabrina closed her eyes to shut out the dizzying display of colors whizzing by, then almost lost her grip on the cat when she landed on something very soft. She sank and then was tossed upward from a giant, squishy trampoline. She opened her eyes after she stopped bouncing.

Glassy-eyed, Val felt her wrist for her pulse. "Oh, good. I'm alive."

"I am *never* taking an elevator again." Libby patted her chest to still her pounding heart.

"Yeah." Looking slightly stunned, Harvey flopped on his back. "I think I just lost any remote inclination I had to try sky-diving."

Still clinging to his strap, Mr. Kraft gasped. "And I thought *teenagers* were going to turn my hair gray before my time."

"Look on the bright side, Mr. Kraft." Sabrina shrugged with an encouraging smile. "Compared to this, teenagers don't seem so bad, right?"

"At the risk of bursting your bubble of misguided cheer, Sabrina, nothing is more dangerous to a middle-aged bachelor's health and well-being than a teenager. And that includes tarantulas, great white sharks, the T-Rex, and my mother."

Sabrina nodded curtly. "I stand corrected."

"Now then!" Strutting across the bouncy landing pad, Fergus waved the rainbow door open. "Shall we?"

"Like we have a choice?" Libby asked hopefully.

"What choice?" Harvey rose and wobbled on the unstable surface. "That's like trying to pick between extra homework and detention. You're in trouble either way."

"So we might as well go for the unknown and be surprised." Val smiled weakly.

"I used to love surprises," Salem sobbed.

One by one the Westbridge wanderers stumbled across the giant pillow and out into a rolling, grassy meadow.

"When are we this time?" Sabrina asked.

"Seventeen hundred B.C.," Fergus answered nonchalantly. "Right after the Milesian Celts from Spain landed and won this land from the Tuatha de Danaan."

"From Lugh's descendants?" Val frowned. "What happened to them?"

"That's what he'd like to know." Fergus gestured toward a solitary figure standing on a high rise. Lost in a deep contemplation, the tall man did not notice them at first.

"Is that another one of your relatives?" Harvey asked.

"No," Fergus said, "although I wouldn't mind to be callin' Amergin kin. He's the most revered Bard poet of the Celtic people. And the one who must give you permission to pass from this time."

"That's not going to be easy." Libby's brow furrowed with concern. "He looks as if he were just unanimously elected geek of the year. Totally bummed."

"Aye and he is that, lass. After the Celts defeated the Tuatha de Danaan, the Danaan just vanished. Poof!" Fergus chuckled.

"I fail to see the humor in that, Fergus." Mr.

Kraft scanned the meadow that sloped downhill beyond Amergin's position.

"Oh, don't be worryin' about the Danaan! They just used their magic to make themselves invisible. Like this!" To demonstrate, Fergus disappeared, then popped back standing in front of Amergin, who apparently couldn't see him.

"There are times I wish I could do that," Val said.

"It's a handy trick, all right." Sabrina smiled.

Libby glanced at both girls and nodded sympathetically. "If I was one of the foremost freaks at Westbridge High, I'd want to become invisible, too."

"Careful, Sabrina." Salem shifted in Sabrina's arms. "I think Libby's bonding."

"Which is about as welcome as Super Glue on the seat of your pants." Setting Salem on the ground, Sabrina got the others back on track. "I'm not really thrilled about getting back on the rainbow-that-runs-rampant-through-time, but it's our only way home, and we need Amergin's permission to leave."

"Let's go." Bolstered by his successful encounter with Lugh, Mr. Kraft led the way across the meadow.

Amergin graced the group with a casual glance as they trudged up the incline. Then he turned his despondent attention back to the deserted land. "Gone! They're just gone!"

Sitting on the crest of the rise, Fergus doubled

over laughing. "Ah, but it's a grand joke the sidhe played on those conquering Celts!"

" 'She'?" Perplexed, Harvey looked at Sabrina. "Who is 'she'?"

"I think that's how you pronounce the Gaelic word *sidhe*—s-i-d-h-e—the magic people."

"Excuse me, Mr. Amergin." Mr. Kraft paused when the poet didn't respond, then tugged on his sleeve. "I hate to interrupt, but if you'd just grant us permission to pass, we'll be on our way and—"

Amergin ignored him. "How could they all just vanish? What have we done?"

Rolling her eyes, Libby walked past the poet to join Fergus higher up the slope. She stopped dead and yelled back. "Hey! You have *got* to see this!"

Chapter 9

☆

Curious, Amergin followed when everyone raced up the hill. He stood behind them on the summit, his eyes narrowed in puzzlement.

"That is incredible!" Val clapped her hands. "The Danaan aren't gone!"

Sabrina stared at the scene below in genuine wonder. A sprawling palace with tall spires that glittered in the sun stood in the lower meadow. Thick ivy clung to crystalline walls and patches of wildflower color lined the walkways and court-yards. Young and beautiful men and women wandered through exotic gardens or danced to merry tunes played on golden harps.

"It's like the fairy lands I used to read about when I was a kid." Harvey grinned.

" 'Fairy tales can come true, mmmphffff'' Salem sang in his crooning baritone.

Libby clamped a hand over his feline mouth. "In the pound no one can hear you sing."

"Are you all daft?" Amergin peered at the lower meadow over Sabrina's shoulder, then backed up a step.

"Are you blind?" Mr. Kraft waved his hand in front of Amergin's face. "The missing Danaan are right there!"

The poet blinked and pushed Mr. Kraft's hand away. "All I see is a large, grass-covered mound, the ruins of an ancient fortress built by a people that passed on long ago."

"You're putting us on, right?" Val asked.

"No, wait!" Sabrina slapped her forehead. "Amergin really can't see them. We can because we all ate the real shamrock baked into Aunt Hilda's cookies!"

"Really?" Val cocked her head. "I knew there was a logical explanation for all this Irish weirdness."

"But poor Amergin's nay got a clue." Fergus danced a jig around the bewildered poet to prove he was invisible to the bard. "The sidhe did not withdraw from Ireland but chose to retreat into their magic realm."

Amergin stared at Mr. Kraft. "You ask permission to pass, stranger. Prove to me that the Tuatha de Danaan have not fled this land, and I'll grant your request."

"No problem!" Harvey fell to the ground on all

95

fours, then glanced up at Sabrina. "All we have to do is find some shamrock for him to eat, right?"

"Right!" Sabrina nodded. The solution seemed simple enough, except that after crawling around the meadow for an hour, no one found any of the large, distinctive clover that was indigenous to the Emerald Isle.

"There might be another way," Fergus finally said. "Especially since there's no shamrock to be found just yet."

"Now he tells us!" Standing up, Libby rubbed her grass-stained knees and glared down at the leprechaun. "For a short, puny old coot who has to stand on tiptoe to reach a doorknob, you really should be more careful whom you push too far!"

"Oh, is that so?" Folding his arms, Fergus glared back. "For someone who thinks jumping up and down and chanting ridiculous rhymes because a bunch of brawny boys get a funny-looking ball from point A to point B, you should be more careful whom *you* insult!"

"Go, Fergus!" Sabrina nudged the furious cheerleader. "Take it from me, Libby. You do not want to tangle with the little guy."

"Enough of this bickering!" Holding his aching back, Mr. Kraft got to his feet. "We're stuck here unless we can prove to Amergin that the Tuatha de Danaan haven't left."

"Come on, Fergus," Val pleaded. "Libby didn't really mean it. Did you Libby?"

Libby indignantly squared her shoulders. "I meant every word! But I'm sorry I said it."

"If you want to find King Kevin's gold, I'd accept that, Fergus," Sabrina said. "That's as close to groveling for forgiveness as Libby's gonna get."

"Perhaps, but I'll have a bit of retribution first, if you don't mind." Fergus snapped his fingers. A stream of golden dust cascaded over Libby, and a giant toadstool appeared.

Crying out in alarm because she couldn't stop herself, Libby kissed Fergus on the forehead. Then she jumped onto the toadstool and danced a jig. She collapsed on the grass when the toadstool suddenly disappeared out from under her.

"Hey! Libby just kissed a leprechaun and danced a jig on a toadstool!" Val looked at the stricken cheerleader hopefully. "Does that mean I can be in the parade?"

"In your dreams!" Fuming, Libby stumbled to her feet.

"Now then." Fergus motioned them all into a huddle. "You'll just have to convince one of the Danaan to reveal himself or herself to Amergin."

"Why don't you just reveal yourself, Fergus?" Harvey asked.

"Because that's against the rainbow rules. And even if I could, do I look like the magic people of this time?"

Far from it, Sabrina thought. The sidhe of long ago were tall, beautiful young people—not "short, puny old coots," as Libby had so accurately pointed out. The glorious Tuatha de Danaan had been sabotaged by cultural prejudice. *No wonder Fergus is so cranky!* Sabrina thought. *Over the years he's come to look like a greeting card.*

"No, I don't, more's the pity of it," Fergus continued. "Sure and Amergin would not accept the sight of me as proof. And I won't risk having the sidhe see what they've become in the millennia ahead."

"So you're suggesting that we march on down to Fairyville and tap a magic person on the shoulder?" Mr. Kraft's eyes widened skeptically. Then he looked up with a goofy expression and spoke as though he were talking to one of the sidhe. "Say there. Would you mind showing yourself to that Celtic invader who just whipped your butt and stole your land?"

"Well, lad—" Fergus rubbed his bearded chin. "It's either that or stay here, thirty-seven hundred years before the invention of computer games, hot tubs, and remote controls."

Mr. Kraft frowned. "I can live without computer games and hot tubs, but—"

Amergin shouldered his way into the huddle. "And who would you be talkin' to?"

Salem wiggled between Sabrina's legs. "Would you believe, the cat?"

Amergin didn't react. Apparently Salem was invisible to him, too.

"Okay." Sabrina straightened up. "The sooner we go, the sooner we can tempt fate on the rampaging rainbow again."

Sitting on the hill beside Amergin, Fergus waved. "And if you don't return, I'll send your regards to your families!"

Sabrina called back over her shoulder. "Don't you have a shoe to make or something?"

It was an easy downhill walk and the sidhe were completely unconcerned with their presence—until they entered the palace gates.

"Ostentatious much?" Libby sneered as she glanced up at the spectacular spires and vine-covered palace walls.

Mr. Kraft approached a young woman sitting in the courtyard. "Pardon me, miss. If I could have a moment—"

Startled, the woman raised her hand, immobilizing Mr. Kraft and Libby. Mr. Kraft froze with his mouth open and his hand extended. Libby's arms were crossed and her nose was wrinkled with disdain.

"I'd say you captured their essences perfectly." Sabrina nodded with a tight smile.

Astounded, the woman stared at Sabrina, Salem, Harvey, and Val. "Are ye magic people or innocents?"

"That depends on which answer will get us turned into garden decorations." Salem leaped into Sabrina's arms.

"I'm innocent. I swear!" Val raised her right

hand. "Of everything except wanting to be cool at any cost."

"Does a parking ticket count?" Harvey asked.

A flawless beauty with long, blond hair, the woman rose and bowed slightly. "I am Eriu, wife of the Danaan king."

Sabrina extended her free hand. "Sabrina. A witch from Westbridge, Massachusetts."

"I see." Eriu inclined her head slightly instead of shaking hands, then arched a perfect eyebrow. "I've not heard of that kingdom."

"It's a little off the beaten track at the moment," Sabrina said.

"What a fabulous place! Is it okay if I look around?" Val's eyes widened with childlike anticipation. "I mean, this is almost as enchanting as the Magic Kingdom at Disney World. Except it doesn't have any rides. Does it?"

"You wouldn't have a snack bar or anything, would you?" Harvey rubbed his stomach. "I'm starved."

Eriu waved Val away and pointed Harvey toward a chicken roasting on a nearby spit.

"Would you mind changing them back?" Sabrina nodded toward the life-size Mr. Kraft and Libby statues. "I know they're both antagonistic and arrogant and impossible to like, but I am responsible for them being here. Sort of."

"Then your magic isn't powerful enough to undo mine?" Eriu asked with guarded curiosity.

"Now, there's a question that may not bear closer examination," Salem said.

"Would you excuse us for just a sec?" Sabrina stepped to the side and lowered her voice. "Gee, Salem. Thanks for the vote of confidence."

"Have you ever been able to shut down Libby or Mr. Kraft?"

"No," Sabrina admitted. "But only because the Other Realm has all those rules and regulations about what I can and cannot do! Apparently, the sidhe don't have any lame mortal management restrictions."

"Which may be why you do!" Salem sighed. "Just beware, okay? Remember what happened with Lugh."

"Don't worry! I can handle it!"

"I think I'll get down. I don't want to get caught in the crossfire." Leaping from Sabrina's arms, Salem sniffed. "Chicken is good. And Harvey's a softie . . ."

As Salem wandered off to beg for tasty morsels, Sabrina turned back and smiled at the Danaan queen. Raising her finger, she pointed at Libby and Mr. Kraft.

"Vice-principal, cheerleader, stiff as a board,
with a flick of my finger to normal restored."

Sabrina flicked.
Nothing happened.
"Don't tell me I forgot to clean it again!"

Pretending to be peeved, Sabrina inspected her finger and blew on it. Obviously the Danaan's magical powers had not diminished in the two centuries since Lugh. Shaking her finger, Sabrina took a deep breath. "Let me just try that again."

"As you wish." Eriu sighed, unimpressed.

Sabrina pointed and closed her eyes to concentrate.

"Come on, you guys, this isn't funny!
Return to find King Kevin's money!"

Opening one eye, Sabrina winced. Libby and Mr. Kraft were still statues. "Oops."

"I like the cat," Eriu said. "He's amusing and furry, but you're getting tiresome."

"Actually, it takes a lot of people time to warm up to me." Laughing nervously, Sabrina flinched, then ducked as Eriu waved her magic arm.

Sabrina was instantly frozen in a stooped position with her hands in front of her face. However, although she couldn't move, she could still see and hear everything that was going on.

Great. That means Mr. Kraft heard me call him antagonistic, arrogant, and unlikable. With luck, maybe he'll take that as a compliment.

Unfortunately, since her magic wasn't powerful enough to release them, she might never have to deal with the wrath of Mr. Kraft again.

Chapter 10

☆

☆

Tucking her violin case under her arm, Hilda dashed toward the chaos erupting around the Westbridge High float. Zelda followed on her heels with the bodhran in her hand and the empty case slung over her shoulder. Instantly taken with the drum, she had refused to let Hilda zap it away.

"Don't panic!" Hilda ran up to Mrs. Quick, who was holding the cookie plate above her head and looking down in alarm. Since she wasn't under the influence of shamrock, Hilda couldn't see the wee folk that were surrounding the stricken math teacher.

"Who are you people?" The math teacher jerked back a couple steps. "Leave my shoes alone! Scat!"

"Just try to stay calm." Hilda smiled reassuringly at Mrs. Quick and reached for the cookie plate. "I can explain this."

"I'm hallucinating, right?" Mrs. Quick blinked, then stumbled backward. The shamrock cookies slid off the plate.

Hilda ducked around Mrs. Quick to catch them, but she wasn't fast enough. She stamped her foot in exasperation as the remaining shamrock cookies fell into tiny invisible hands and disappeared into invisible mouths. "Are you guys totally against the concept of sharing?"

"They're laughing." Scowling, Mrs. Quick retreated to a nearby park bench and sat down.

"What are they doing now?" Hilda asked.

"Storming the float." Mrs. Quick's eyes rolled upward and she fainted.

"No! Don't do that." Sagging with dismay, Hilda propped up the teacher and patted her cheek to revive her.

Zelda dropped the bodhran and case by the bench and raced to the float, where six hysterical cheerleaders were huddled on the low section in front of the goalposts and tiers.

"Get away! Get away!" Jill squealed as one of the leprechauns lifted a green and white pompom and shook it in her face.

"It's okay, girls!" Zelda waved her hands in a calming motion, hoping no one near the float noticed the pompom wiggling in midair. "They're just curious and want to party!"

"Not!" Cee Cee grimaced as she looked down.

"No way, buster! I don't date old guys who only come up to my knees!"

"Especially ones who get their clothes off the rack at the costume shop!" Jill grabbed the pom-pom and held it above her head, then lunged toward the goalposts as the football suddenly separated from the wire. "Give that back!"

Hilda sighed as the football sailed through the air into unseen waiting arms. The ball, carried by a fleet and invisible leprechaun, zoomed across the parking lot with Jill and Cee Cee in hot pursuit.

Recovering from their initial shock, the rest of the cheerleaders desperately tried to retrieve the flowers and cardboard shamrocks other wee folk were quickly removing from the float and tossing in the air.

"Stop that this instant!" Zelda issued the order with a dark scowl.

"This one wants to know why he should listen to you." Crystal Logue, a senior, batted away the invisible hand that suddenly untied her sneakers.

"Because if he doesn't," Zelda said, "you won't let them ride on your float in the parade!"

"Ride on our float? I don't think so!" Jennifer, Crystal's younger sister, tugged on a shamrock floating before her. The decoration ripped into two pieces. "Now look what you've done!"

When Mrs. Quick came to, Hilda patted her hand. "Why don't you just sit here and rest for a while? With your eyes closed."

Nodding, Mrs. Quick closed her eyes and took a deep breath. "I'm seeing leprechauns!"

"Well, yes, you are. But—it is St. Patrick's Day."

"And that explains it?" Mrs. Quick opened her eyes and muffled a cry as the leprechaun running the football leaped over the bench.

Cee Cee and Jill darted around the ends of the bench and tackled him as he landed. "Gotcha!"

"I think I need a nap." Mrs. Quick passed out again.

"That'll work." Hilda eased the woman's upper body down on the bench and looked at the girls behind her.

Jill frowned, her gaze focused on the ground. "Is that three wishes each, Patrick?"

"Or do we each get one and have to share the third?" Cee Cee asked, then pouted. "Only three between us? What a rip-off!"

Confident that the captured leprechaun could keep the girls from wishing for anything more disastrous than perpetual summer vacation at Westbridge High, Hilda rushed to the float.

Zelda whistled to get everyone's attention. "Are they listening?"

"Most of them are." Jennifer started, then caught the football that came flying back onto the float trailing golden dust.

One wish down, Hilda thought.

"All of them except this one!" Crystal placed her hands over several rustling flowers and glowered at the leprechaun trying to pull them off the wire foundation. "Pay attention!"

"All right, then," Zelda said firmly. "This is the deal."

While Zelda negotiated a truce between the Irish Mischief Makers and the Westbridge Scallion cheerleaders, Hilda scanned the parking lot looking for other disturbances.

A man in a green suit was changing a flat tire on the parade marshall's car. When he reached for the lug nuts, they were gone. Three volunteer firemen were trying to secure a giant shamrock on top of their ladder truck. Every time they got it sitting straight, it tipped to the left again. The tuba player in the high school marching band pulled a wadded-up newspaper out of his horn. A well-dressed woman from the Ladies Auxiliary chased her hat across the pavement. Whenever she got close, it "blew" away again.

"At least the wee folk are having fun." Sighing, Hilda turned to check on Mrs. Quick. A movement by the Woodland Scout float stopped her in her tracks. One of her shamrock cookies appeared out of nowhere and settled beside the scout leader's hand. Curious, the man picked it up.

The leprechauns hadn't eaten them. They were passing them out!

"No! Wait! Don't—" Hilda started to run just as the man popped the cookie into his mouth.

Clapping her hand over her eyes, Hilda watched between parted fingers as the man jumped, looked around in panic, then fled through the park shouting at the top of his lungs.

"Leprechauns! They're everywhere!"

"Ohmigosh!" A woman raced out of the park rest room. "She has wings!"

"Now what's going on?" Zelda stepped up beside Hilda.

"Nothing much." Hilda shrugged. "Does our mal-magic insurance cover inciting a riot by cookies?"

"Eriu! Eriu!" Shouting, Val ran back into the courtyard.

Peeking over the top of her hand, which had been immobilized blocking her face, Sabrina couldn't tell what Val was carrying. Val whipped the object behind her back when she noticed Sabrina's petrified condition.

Munching a chicken leg, Harvey ambled up behind Val with Salem trotting at his heels.

Val stared at Sabrina. "Was it something she said?"

"It matters not," Eriu said, smiling warmly at Val.

It matters a lot! Sabrina thought frantically.

Harvey leaned over and rapped on Sabrina's hard head with his knuckles. "Sabrina? Are you okay?"

Just fine, Harvey! For a rock!

Salem sat in front of her and looked up. "Considering the way you handled this, the Witches'

Council may revoke your license on the grounds of diplomatic incompetence."

"And what can I be doin' for you?" Eriu asked Val.

"Uh—I, uh—" Val's hand shook as she pulled a potted shamrock from behind her back. "It's about this plant—"

Plant? Sabrina did a mental double-take. She knew they needed the shamrock to convince Amergin the invisible magic people were still on the island. However, getting the poet's permission to continue on their rainbow way wouldn't save her or Mr. Kraft and Libby. As things stood now, their best prospect for the future was holding down pedestals in museums.

"It's really exquisite," Val gushed. "Distinctive, you know?"

"I do." Eriu's beautiful face lit up with the radiance of her delighted smile. "Before the invaders came, I was plannin' to spread this enchanted clover throughout the whole island."

"You're kidding." Val threw up her free hand and shook her head surprised wonder. "Would you believe that's exactly what I was thinking!"

Eriu's smile faded. "But I'll not be giving the shamrock to the Celts. Nay, not even to Amergin, who mourns us. The sidhe became invisible on purpose! So the Celts could thrive here without feeling threatened."

"But the Irish aren't going to eat shamrock!" Val protested.

"Except on really rare occasions," Harvey added. "If it gets baked into cookies by accident or something."

"And what would they be doing with it, then?" Eriu asked curiously.

"Uh—" Val faltered.

"Wait! I know this one!" Stepping forward, Salem raised his tail and looked wistfully into space. "It becomes a symbol of Ireland's magical heritage, recognized and honored throughout the world."

"And how would you be knowin' that?" Eriu smiled, amused.

"I'm a cat! I know everything." Salem's tail flicked back and forth. "I even know that they call this island Erin—after *you!*"

"And this is truth you're speakin'?" Eriu eyed Salem pointedly.

"Is it?" Harvey asked.

"Would I lie?" Salem looked shocked.

Only when it suits you, Sabrina thought. In this case, however, Salem was stating fact.

"It's absolutely true!" Val nodded vigorously. "And we'd be more than happy to plant some of it out there right now. Except—"

Sabrina perked up.

"Yes?" Eriu looked puzzled.

"We could make a lot more progress if *all* of us returned to do the planting." Val's gaze flicked toward Sabrina, Libby, and Mr. Kraft.

Cool move, Val!

Eriu paused to consider it, then sighed. "All right. I'll free them. But only because the Danaan must not be forgotten."

When Eriu waved her arm, Sabrina, Libby, and Mr. Kraft immediately returned to normal.

Furious, Libby sputtered. "How dare—"

Mr. Kraft clamped his hand over her mouth. "One more word and it's detention for the rest of your life."

Taking the hint, Sabrina just smiled tightly at Eriu and pocketed her magical pointing finger.

A short while later, their arms laden with potted shamrock, everyone returned to the hill where Amergin and Fergus were keeping vigil. While the others spread out to plant the enchanted clover in the meadow, Sabrina offered a handful of shamrock leaves to Amergin.

"Eriu sent it," Sabrina explained. "If you eat it, you'll be able to see the Tuatha de Danaan's palace by that mound."

Frowning uncertainly, Amergin stuffed the green leaves into his mouth, chewed, and swallowed. Within a few seconds his despairing countenance changed to an expression of pure rapture.

"The Danaan . . ." He sighed.

"So! Can we go now?" Sabrina asked.

Amergin just nodded again, his gaze fastened on the faery palace below.

"Assuming that's a yes, we'll just be on our way."

Fergus appeared in front of her and raised a

warning finger. "But not until you've done keepin' your promise to the Danaan queen to get the shamrock settled in."

"No problem. I won't be ready for another heart-stopping spin on Space Rainbow until my arms limber up enough to hang on!" Rubbing her stiff shoulder, Sabrina joined the others.

When the planting was completed and they were finally assembled inside the rainbow again, everyone gritted their teeth and hung on to their straps for dear life.

The rainbow didn't jerk, swoop, or even shudder.

"Okay, Fergus! What's going on?" Sabrina asked.

"Well and I'll tell ya." Fergus hooked his arm through his strap and dangled by the crook in his elbow. "In case you hadn't noticed, this particular rainbow is a bit peculiar."

"You *think?*" Libby snapped. "Tell us something we don't know."

"And seein' as how you're all ready for whatever it's plannin' next, there's no thrill a'tall for it."

"So what would you be meaning by that, then?" Realizing she had adopted the leprechaun's Irish lilt and manner, Sabrina rephrased. "What's that supposed to mean?"

Fergus giggled. "You just have to give it a fair chance to catch you by surprise."

"Oh! You mean like this!" Harvey raised both

hands above his head like a daring roller-coaster rider.

The escalator stairs suddenly appeared and began to move upward at a sedate, department store pace.

"And sometimes it takes it's own sweet time. Or so I've heard tell." Fergus frowned. "Which is no fun a'tall, if you ask me."

"We didn't." Tensing, Salem secured his grip on Sabrina's shirt.

"This rainbow has had a pretty tough day," Val said. "Maybe it's just tired."

"Then again—" Standing in front and above everyone else, Mr. Kraft moaned as the moving stairs flattened, then formed carnival ride cars around them. "I don't think I'm gonna like this."

Everyone dropped into hard seats and safety bars locked into place a split second before the connected multicolored cars crested the incline. With its captive passengers screaming, the rainbow roller coaster swooped downward and into the first banked turn of a ride that made Sabrina wonder if her teeth would survive intact.

Chapter 11

☆

☆

Sold out!" Hilda glared at the elderly merchant behind the counter in the florist shop. "How can you be sold out of shamrock plants?"

The man scratched behind his ear. "The fact that it's St. Patrick's Day might have *something* to do with it."

"Now what am I supposed to do?" Hilda leaned against the counter. Since shamrock had magical properties, it wasn't something she could just zap up with a flick of her finger. The practical-joking leprechauns were making sure she and Zelda didn't get any of the snitched shamrock cookies they were handing out to parade participants. Now she wished she had taken Zelda's advice and just popped herself to Ireland to restock.

"If I don't get some real shamrock soon, Westbridge will be toothpicks by nightfall!" Hilda added hotly.

"You're pulling my leg, right?" The old man chuckled.

"Now *there's* an idea. I haven't given anyone a case of elastic legs in a while. . . ." Restraining herself, Hilda took a deep breath. "Is there anywhere else in town I can get some? In the state? That you know of? I just need a handful of leaves!"

"Tell me why you want them. The shamrock leaves, I mean."

"So we can see the wee folk!" Hilda answered, as though that should be obvious. "Zelda and I can't possibly get those little Irish twerps under control if they're invisible to us!"

The man didn't even blink. "Shamrock does that, huh?"

"Yes. But you didn't hear that from me!" She dashed from the store. As she ran by the window, she saw the man pick up a cookie that had just appeared on the counter and put it in his mouth. She paused just long enough to see him grab a broom and swat at the leprechaun dancing a jig across his countertop.

"And everyone thinks the United States has never been invaded by a foreign power."

The rainbow riders stumbled out of the colorful, arched mist.

Sinking to his knees in the weeds by a narrow dirt road, Mr. Kraft wrapped his arms around his trembling body and rocked back and forth. "I don't know how much more of this I can take, Fergus. My life has passed before my eyes so many times today, I'm remembering things that didn't happen!"

"There now, Mr. Kraft." Fergus patted his shoulder. "There's only but a couple thousand more years to cover."

"How many years per hour does that thing go anyway?" Harvey waved toward the rainbow.

"Does it matter?" Sabrina asked, recognizing a leading male question. "I'm sure it doesn't need a supercharged thingamabob or anything."

"Irrelevant," Val said. "Every boy I've ever known can find something to improve on a car or a computer whether it needs improving or not."

"I remember." Salem sighed. "I had this thing about getting better gas mileage from a tank. And I would have, too, if Drell hadn't caught me trying to take over the world."

"Some things never change." Fergus pointed down the road. "That young fella over there is always tinkerin' with his chariot."

The young man stood in the middle of the road with his back turned toward them. Even though Sabrina couldn't see his face, his long hair, broad shoulders, and bearing exuded an essence of confidence and power. He seemed to sense their presence and glanced back.

"He's just as handsome as Lugh." Impressed, Libby smiled and waved.

The man scowled back.

"And he apparently has good taste," Sabrina quipped.

"Sure and it's no wonder the lad looks the spittin' image of Lugh," Fergus said proudly. "Lugh of the long arm is Cuchulain's father. He is and that's a fact."

"Coo who?" Harvey asked.

"Coo-cuh-len." Fergus pronounced the ancient Celtic name slowly. "Another of Ireland's most heroic figures."

"But Lugh lived almost two thousand years ago," Val said.

"Aye, but he's of the Danaan and beyond the touch of time. And it's his son, Cuchulain, whose permission you'll be needin' to pass here." With that settled, Fergus clapped his hands together. "So shall we be getting' on with it, then?"

Libby took the lead with Fergus as the group advanced down the road toward the wary young warrior. Thick forests rose on both sides of the narrow track, casting dark and ominous shadows over the scene.

"Couldn't we at least have a hint about the potential calamity we're walking into now, Fergus?" Libby asked.

"Sure and it's soon enough you'll be findin' that out." Skipping ahead, Fergus sat on a log to watch.

Cuchulain turned to face the rest of the group with his spear in hand. "Halt right there!"

The rainbow riders stopped dead five feet in front of the serious young man with a deep, commanding voice that matched the look of determination in his eyes.

"You'll be goin' no farther down the road to Ulster today, people of Connacht." To emphasize this statement, Cuchulain raised his spear over his shoulder.

"Connacht?" Sabrina glanced at the leprechaun.

"Cuchulain is of the Red Branch, the honored line that rules over Ulster," Fergus explained. "Connacht is a rival kingdom."

"Why am I not happy to hear that?" Sabrina muttered.

"Because he thinks we're from Connacht." Harvey nodded toward Cuchulain.

"No!" Mr. Kraft shook his head and frantically waved his hands. "We're from Westbridge! In a country far, far away that hasn't even been discovered yet!"

"I wouldn't be knowin' of that, but you're comin' up the road from Connacht." Cuchulain's piercing eyes narrowed. "The nine-day Curse of Macha is upon the men of Ulster. King Conor mac Nessa has set me the task of delayin' Queen Maeve's foray into his lands to steal the Brown Bull of Quelgny until those days have passed. And I will—with my life."

"And I think he means it." Salem rubbed against Sabrina's leg. "I am *so* glad he can't see me."

"A cow?" Val eyed Cuchulain in disbelief. "Your two kingdoms are fighting over a cow?"

"The Brown Bull is not a cow!" Cuchulain bristled. "Sure and you know that if Queen Maeve has the bull, her wealth will be equal to her husband's and her position of power in Connacht will be secure."

"Really?" Libby's interest in power was instantly aroused.

"I'm a little concerned about this curse business." Mr. Kraft shifted his gaze between Fergus and Cuchulain.

"Aye and I know you can't hail from Ulster because ye not be a'bed with the pain," Cuchulain said. "I am of the Danaan and did not succumb."

"Pain?" Mr. Kraft asked cautiously. "Like in hangnail? Stubbing your toe?"

Fergus laughed. "After her husband bragged about her speed afoot to the king of Ulster, Macha was forced to race the king's horses, even though she was soon to deliver a child. For revenge, Macha cursed the men of Ulster with the pain of birthing whenever they faced great danger. Such as now."

"Good for Macha!" Libby's eyes flashed defiantly as she turned on Cuchulain. "Sounds to me

119

as if the men of Ulster deserve to be invaded! And I, for one, have more sympathy for Queen Maeve's position."

Cuchulain tensed, his hand flexing on his spear.

"Stuff it, Libby!" Sabrina took a bold step toward Cuchulain. "I think a little clarification is called for here, don't you?"

"I'm totally confused." Harvey shrugged apologetically.

Cuchulain hesitated.

"Okay." Sabrina took quick advantage of the opening. "Queen Maeve from Connacht is about to invade Ulster to steal a bull. The men of Ulster can't stop her because they're incapacitated by Macha's curse. You're not, so the king sent you to delay Queen Maeve's army for nine days all by yourself. Does that about cover it?"

Cuchulain nodded. "Except for how I'm going to prevent the entire Connacht army's advance and what you're doin' here."

Val pointed into the forest where the rainbow was barely visible through the trees. "Actually, we need your permission to get back on that rainbow over there."

Noting Cuchulain's baffled reaction, Sabrina clarified again. "Which brought us here to *help* you!"

"I'm not helping him!" Folding her arms, Libby stubbornly raised her chin. "No way. Why shouldn't Macha get her revenge and Maeve strike a blow for women's rights, huh? I mean, I can't believe you're on his side!"

"Sure and I wish I could tie your treacherous tongue in a knot!" Cuchulain roared.

Libby flinched.

"I could arrange that!" Sabrina wagged her finger. "But the rest of us would like to get back to the twentieth century!"

"Yeah!" Val scowled. "We're missing the parade!"

"Not that I mind that," Harvey said.

"'Treacherous tongue.'" Mr. Kraft laughed shortly. "I'll have to remember that one."

"Silence!" Cuchulain bellowed.

Everyone shut up and watched nervously as Cuchulain began to pace back and forth. He stopped, looked up suddenly, and smiled at Libby.

"Aye and you're a troublesome wench I'd not want to be havin' on my side, but you've given me a grand idea!"

"She did? Did I miss something?" Harvey blinked when Cuchulain handed him the spear.

"Mind that well, lad. It belonged to Lugh himself." Cuchulain sprinted into the trees.

"Wait!" Sabrina hollered. "We'd really like to get moving!"

"I don't. I want to see what he's going to do." Val walked over to the log and sat down beside Fergus.

Since they couldn't leave until Cuchulain granted them permission, Sabrina, Salem, Mr. Kraft, and Harvey joined Val and the leprechaun.

Libby moved to the far side of the road. "I'm never speaking to any of you again!"

"Hey!" Sabrina brightened. "I knew there had to be an upside to all this."

"Shh!" Salem flopped on the end of the log.

A rustling on the edge of the forest snagged everyone's attention. Standing on one foot, Cuchulain pulled an oak sapling out of the ground by the roots.

"I am definitely glad we're on his side," Mr. Kraft said.

"I don't get it." Harvey shook his head as the young Celt carried the tree into the middle of the road.

With a lightning movement, the Danaan tied the sapling into a knot with one hand, then sank the rooted end into the road. Using a knife, he carved something into the Connacht side of the sapling. When he was done, he came smiling back to the group. "The road is now impassable to Queen Maeve's men."

"Impassable?" Val nibbled her lip. "I don't know how to tell you this, Kook, but that little tree isn't gonna stop an army."

Cuchulain threw his head back and laughed. "No, but the geis on it will."

"The what?" Val asked.

"A geis is an obligation that all Celts are honor bound to obey," Fergus explained. "They would die rather than break one."

"Aye and I doubt any one of Maeve's men can duplicate that feat exactly as I did." A sly grin dawned on Cuchulain's face. "And someone must in order to pass down the road."

"Speaking of passing," Sabrina said. "Do we have your permission to leave?"

Rubbing his chin, Cuchulain eyed them all narrowly. "Such inspiring folk are not easily found and the Red Branch may be needin' you again. So why should I be sendin' you on your way?"

"Uh—because she's a witch!" Val pointed at Sabrina.

Cuchulain started, then laughed. "A witch, are you, then? And why should I be fearin' a bit of a thing like you? Who can do no more than tie ritual knots in string and breathe on them to cast a wee spell?"

Sabrina had learned about primitive string magic while studying to get her witch's license. Wannabe Celtic witches had practiced the amusing art, but it was a party trick compared to the real thing.

Sabrina smiled. "Because I can do this!"

Raising her finger, she fired off several quick points. Thunder boomed and lightning flashed, although the skies were clear. A ring of fire suddenly blazed around the knotted sapling in the road, and the branches of the huge oaks lining the track wove themselves into Celtic knots.

"That's why." Mr. Kraft gave Cuchulain his sternest vice-principal look over the rim of his glasses.

"Have a safe journey." Waving, Cuchulain retrieved his spear from Harvey and backed off.

After removing her spells, Sabrina led the way back to the rainbow. Libby silently followed at a distance. When they were all aboard, everyone grabbed for their straps.

The rainbow balked again.

They avoided looking at one another until Libby finally snapped.

"Okay! Somebody has to let go."

"That was a short, but sweet cold-shoulder treatment," Sabrina muttered.

"My stomach hurts." Val doubled over, clutching her midsection with her free hand.

"Don't look at me," Harvey said. "Once was enough."

"Well, I'm certainly not going to." Mr. Kraft tightened his grip. "Vice-principal's privilege."

"I'm not a'tall sure the rainbow has any respect for age or position, Mr. Kraft." Fergus's expression was serious, but his eyes twinkled merrily.

"Tough. I'm not letting gooooooooooooooooo-ooo—"

Sabrina stared in rapt fascination as Mr. Kraft suddenly rocketed up and out of sight as though he'd been shot from a canon. Strap and all.

Chapter 12

☆

Hilda blew her hair out of her face and dug in her heels. She wasn't about to let go of the official Westbridge parade marshall's flag staff for fear the town would never see it again.

The three leprechauns tugging on the other end of the ornate, gold-plated rod were just as determined.

"Let go, you old witch!" The grouchy little man in front let go with one hand just long enough to push his three-cornered hat back on his head.

"I'm not old!" Furious, Hilda pulled harder, yanking the staff from the leprechauns' grasp. She stumbled backward and landed on her butt. "Just clumsy."

The three wee men giggled, bowed, then scampered away.

Standing up, Hilda brushed herself off and

squared her shoulders to recoup some of her lost dignity. However, no one around her had even noticed the embarrassing fall. Everyone who had not eaten shamrock cookies was desperately trying to repair the floats that were mysteriously falling apart. Those who could see the rampaging wee folk were hysterical, numb with shock, or gone.

Brushing her hair back, Hilda headed toward the marshall's car to return the stolen staff. It had carried Old Glory on the lead car in every Westbridge parade for twenty-five years. It wouldn't miss this one, either.

If the sabotaged parade ever got started.

She had no idea if Zelda was making any progress trying to talk the little people into helping rather than hindering the annual Irish event. The fact that so many mortals could see them had apparently spurred the mischievous mini-men on to greater and more disruptive efforts than usual.

"I was better off coping with Fergus." Hilda sighed, wondering what was happening to Sabrina, Willard, and the other Westbridge students Fergus had lured onto the rainbow. She had never been a sucker for the old pot-of-gold scam herself, but she had heard tales of the dangerous journey through Irish history. It was said that most people never returned. And the rainbow pager she had installed in Mr. Kraft's office remained silent.

"There!" someone shouted, interrupting Hilda's disturbed thoughts. "She's got it!"

Hilda looked up to see the mayor running toward her with a police officer—the same officer who had seen Zelda make a wrong turn into a one-way alley.

"I'll take that!" The mayor ripped the flag staff from Hilda's hand, then jumped aside as a large cardboard cutout of a cute, dancing leprechaun toppled off a flatbed truck loaded with local veterans.

The officer glowered at her. "Aren't you a little old to be playing juvenile pranks?"

"I am not old! And for your information"—Hilda glanced at the man's badge—"Officer Murphy, I just recovered that staff from the little—creeps who took it."

"Little creeps?" Murphy glanced around. "What little creeps?"

"The ones who are tearing this parade apart flower by flower!" Hilda's temper flared.

"I don't see anyone but you," the mayor said.

Officer Murphy smiled. "And you're under arrest for the theft of city property."

"Oh, really? Arrest this!" At her wits' end, Hilda stuffed a few of the remaining cookie crumbs in the officer's mouth and pointed to make him swallow. "Now what do you see?"

Murphy blinked. "Leprechauns and faeries. Dozens of 'em!"

"What?" Scowling, the mayor took the crumbs Hilda held out and ate them. "Oh, no. It can't be!"

"Oh, yes, it can be." Hilda clapped her hands to get the flabbergasted men's attention. "And if we don't do something, this parade will never get out of the parking lot!"

"Uh, I can arrest them for disturbing the peace," Murphy said. "Or willful destruction of property, maybe."

"Not a chance," Hilda said. "The wee folk are too fast, too cunning, and they have no respect for authority."

"Hilda!" Zelda waved as she ran across the lot with half a dozen frolicking leprechauns tagging behind her. She was carrying Hilda's violin case. Lurching to a halt, she paused to catch her breath.

And a leprechaun appeared on her back and jumped down.

"Aye and it's a fine day for a parade, isn't it, Mr. Murphy?" The grinning little man tipped his hat and bowed. "And Mr. Mayor."

Hilda recognized Patrick O'Flannigan, the same leprechaun who had stolen Mrs. Atherton's stapler and owed Zelda a favor.

"Uh—" The stunned mayor blinked, but quickly recovered. "There's nothing left intact to parade with!"

"But I think we can fix that," Zelda said. "The little people are marvelous craftsmen."

"Yes, indeed." Patrick puffed out his chest. "The finest craftsmen in the world, we are."

"Patrick assures me that they can put everything back just as quickly as they took it apart so the parade can start on time." Zelda hesitated. "For a price."

"Anything!" The mayor pulled a neatly folded handkerchief from his pocket and wiped his brow.

"That's blackmail!" Murphy scowled.

"What price?" Hilda asked suspiciously.

Zelda smiled tightly. "The wee folk want to ride on all the floats in the parade."

"Done!" The mayor sighed. "I wish all the city's problems could be solved as easily."

"There's more." Zelda shifted awkwardly.

"What more?" Hilda frowned.

"You and I have to ride on the Westbridge High float and play whatever Irish tunes the leprechauns request." Zelda held out Hilda's violin case.

Hilda didn't take it. "No. No way. Not in a zillion years. No."

The mayor gasped. "You must! It's your civic duty."

"No."

"I thought you'd say that. Jill! Cee Cee!" Zelda waved the two reluctant girls forward. "Go ahead."

"Do we have to?" Jill whined.

"Yes!" Zelda eyed them sternly.

Unhappy but compliant, the two girls spoke in unison. "We wish for Hilda Spellman to agree to play any Irish song the leprechauns request on the Westbridge float during the parade."

Hilda paled. *The third wish.*

"Done!" Patrick chuckled and snapped his fingers. A sparkling stream of golden dust flew from his hand.

Hilda ducked, but there was no escape from the magic dust cloud that settled over her. Helpless to resist the leprechaun's wish magic, she took the violin case from Zelda. She would play, but she didn't have to like it!

"All set, Hilda?" Zelda asked cautiously.

"Yeah."

"Okay, then! Patrick!" Grinning, Zelda patted the top of the wee man's hat. "Get your people moving, dear. You've got twenty minutes."

"Sure and we'll be ready!" Moving aside, Patrick conferred with the other five leprechauns, then dispatched them to get the other little people organized and busy.

"What a waste of a perfectly good wish," Jill muttered.

"Our last one, too." Cee Cee kicked a stone.

"Only because you let Patrick trick you into wishing that Ryan Walters would get lost!" Jill rolled her eyes.

"I know." Cee Cee sighed as the girls turned and headed back toward the Westbridge High float, looking for the Westbridge junior class officer. "I wonder where he is?"

"All right!" Hilda snapped as she started after the two cheerleaders. "Let's get this show on the road!"

Jogging to catch up, Zelda beamed. "I'm so

excited. This is going to be so much more fun than just watching the parade. We're going to be in it!"

"We?"

Zelda nodded. "You're playing the fiddle, and I'm playing the bodhran."

Hilda stopped. "Zelda! You don't know how to play the bodhran."

Zelda raised her finger. "I do now!"

Shaking her head, Hilda trudged on, then stopped again when Patrick tugged on her jacket. "What?"

"How about warmin' up with "Paddy McGinty's Goat"?"

"Sure. Why not?" Hilda smiled—with difficulty. "A song about a goat that eats clothes and money. Another classic."

"Sure and 'tis that." Patrick nodded enthusiastically. "And then I'd like to be hearin' me favorite, 'Finnegan's Wake.'"

"Of course," Hilda said through clenched teeth.

It was growing dark when Sabrina and her companions emerged from the rainbow the fourth time.

"I don't know what was worse." Mr. Kraft clung to Libby's arm as he staggered out the door. "Flying faster than a speeding bullet or tumbling out of the catch net."

"Just be grateful it wasn't a boa net." Sabrina squinted in the deepening twilight. Another dirt road ran through the open country beyond the trees on their right. However, she couldn't see clearly in the gathering dusk. "Remind me to work on that night-vision spell when we get home, Salem."

"Sure. If we get home. Which I'm really beginning to doubt."

"What totally incorrigible relative of yours are we going meet this time, Fergus?" Libby asked sarcastically. "You know, if I had your family tree, I'd own a chainsaw."

"Now, there's no need to be insultin' me illustrious ancestors, missy!" Fergus snapped.

"Don't mind her, Fergus." Sabrina smiled warmly. "I think your ancestors are terrific. Lugh was totally cool."

"Cuchulain was more entertaining," Salem said.

"I thought Eriu was sweet." Val sighed wistfully. "Just knowing I actually met the woman Ireland was named for gives me goose bumps."

"It is kind of chilly." Harvey rubbed his hands together. "Where are we, anyway?"

"And when?" Shivering in the brisk evening air, Val wrapped her arms around herself.

"It's the second century and the mound of Tara lies just up the road," Fergus said. "Tara was the heart of Danaan society before the Celts came. Now it's the most revered site in the land and home of King Cormac MacArt. As well as bein' our last stop before the end of the rainbow."

"Thank goodness." Rubbing his temples, Mr. Kraft sat on a large rock. "No amount of gold is worth all this."

"I beg to differ." Salem's eyes gleamed at the thought.

Libby sank down on another rock. "I don't suppose they had portable space heaters in the second century. I'm freezing."

"I don't think they did," Harvey said seriously. "But if I get some wood, we could build a fire! Be right back."

"Sure and that's not a good idea a'tall!" Fergus shouted as Harvey ran into the trees, but Harvey didn't turn back. "It's Samhain."

"It is?" Sabrina shuddered. "No wonder it's cold! Samhain is Halloween," she explained to the others.

"Aye. The night when the way between the Otherworld and the mortal realm is open." Fergus nodded solemnly. "And we really don't want to be attractin' the attention of the goblin Aillen."

"Or this guy, either." Hands above his head, Harvey backed out of the woods. "But I guess it's a little late."

In the lingering gray before nightfall, Sabrina could just make out the huge form of the young man prodding Harvey with the tip of a heavy sword.

Fergus jumped up and down with joy. "Well, if it isn't Fionn MacCumhail himself. Also known as Finn MacCool and the man who must give you permission to pass. Isn't he grand?"

"Totally," Val said, awed.

Sabrina had to agree with Val. Finn was as tall and handsome as Lugh and Cuchulain, but appeared to be several years younger.

"My fingers are getting numb!" Libby pulled her sweater down over her hands.

"The blood's draining from mine. Can I put my arms down now, Mr. Cool?" Harvey asked.

Without relaxing his guard, Finn nodded and motioned for Harvey to move back. Then he silently studied the rest of the rainbow landing party.

"Finn's of Danaan heritage, too, and only seventeen," Fergus announced proudly. "But if he can keep Aillen from destroying the encampment around Tara again tonight, the king will appoint him leader of the fianna, Cormac's elite guard."

"You mean this goblin guy has attacked the mound of Tara before?" Sabrina asked Fergus.

"Aye," Fergus said gravely. "Even the sidhe have evil ones among them. Aillen is a dark force of great power."

Unable to see the leprechaun, Finn brushed past Harvey to confront Sabrina. "What do you know of Aillen?"

"Not a thing." Tangling with an evil goblin was not on Sabrina's to-do list. "Would you mind just giving us permission to continue on our way?"

"And some heat!" Libby's teeth were chattering so hard, her voice shook.

Annoyed by Libby's complaints, Sabrina whirled and pointed. A blazing campfire appeared.

"Bad move!" Fergus's eyes widened in alarm.

"Why?" Sabrina asked, bewildered.

"You are in league with Aillen!" Finn raged.

"Because," Fergus said, "Aillen burns down the king's encampment by hurling fireballs!"

"Nice going, Sabrina." Mr. Kraft threw up his hands and sat down beside Libby.

"She's certainly not pointing a thousand on this trip, that's for sure," Salem said dryly.

"Oops!" Sabrina leveled her finger at Finn when he took a step toward her. "Don't come any closer or I'll fire! No! I didn't mean that! I meant—oh, forget it!" She flicked as Finn lunged.

The huge man fell facefirst onto the hard ground and lay still.

"What did you do?" Val sprang to Finn and gently shook his shoulder. "He's out cold."

"Yes, but I'm still in one piece, if that counts." Casting another deft point, Sabrina doused the campfire.

"Hey!" Libby protested. "I'm not warmed up yet."

"I don't see the problem, Libby," Sabrina said bluntly. "You've never warmed up to anything before."

"And just how are we supposed to get out of here if our pass person is unconscious, hmm?" Mr. Kraft eyed Sabrina coldly. "Preferably before this Gaelic goblin arsonist arrives."

"Finn will come to in a minute." Sabrina waved Mr. Kraft's concern aside and turned to Fergus. "Does he have any chance of defeating Aillen?"

"It hurts me to say it, but no." Fergus shrugged. "Aillen lulls everyone guarding the mound into a sound sleep with a flute before he attacks. No one who hears the music can stay awake."

"Too bad Finn's not deaf." Harvey frowned. "Just for tonight, I mean."

"Harvey!" Sabrina slapped him on the back. "You're brilliant!"

"I am?" Harvey hesitated, then shrugged with a baffled frown. "Thanks."

Moaning, Finn drew himself into a sitting position, then looked up in a panic.

Val quickly sat back. "I was just checking your pulse."

"Just stay calm, MacCool." Sabrina raised a warning finger. "Trust me and you can add 'defeats goblins' to your résumé for that job you want with the king."

Finn cocked his head, obviously intrigued. "And why should I be trustin' the likes of a strange sidhe who calls fire from the air like Aillen?"

"Because I'm the good sidhe of the—uh, fireworks control authority." Sabrina flicked her finger again, producing a hard leather cap with ear flaps. Closing her eyes, she began to chant.

"Cap that's not cool L.A. Gear,
let no sound invade Finn's ears."

Sabrina pointed, completing the spell.

"Do you think you'll ever get the knack of making up a decent rhythm?" Mr. Kraft asked.

"Spells are graded on function, Mr. Kraft, not style." Sabrina handed the cap to Finn. "Put this on. Then go stand over there with your back to us."

The giant Celt slipped on the cap and turned away as Sabrina had instructed.

"Okay, Salem," Sabrina said. "Sing whatever you've been working on with the neighborhood cat chorus."

"Really?" Salem's ears perked forward. "You want me to sing like a cat?"

"Actually, I want to make sure that Finn can't hear anything."

Crestfallen, Salem sighed. Then he began to yowl.

All the humans covered their ears.

Except Finn, who shifted from one foot to the other while he waited in blissful silence.

"Enough!" Sabrina yelled. "Salem! That's enough."

"I think one of my fillings shattered!" Val wailed.

Eyes closed and getting into it, Salem yowled on.

Mr. Kraft jumped to his feet, whipped off his tie, and muffled the cat.

Finn jumped when Sabrina tapped him on the shoulder. "You can turn around now."

Finn blinked, then grinned broadly as he removed the cap. "I didn't hear a word you were sayin'. 'Tis a cap of silence, isn't it?"

"You got it. Wear that and you won't hear Aillen's slumber concerto on the flute tonight, either." Sabrina gave him a thumbs-up. "So can we go now?"

"Go where you would. The king's camp and the mound of Tara are saved." Amazed, Finn turned and walked away without even waving goodbye.

No one from Westbridge said a word as they tramped back to the waiting rainbow. The next stop was the end of the line and King Kevin's pot of gold.

As Sabrina secured Salem and herself inside, she felt a rush of trepidation. She wasn't anxious about whatever stomach-churning, heart-wrenching method of transportation the rainbow was planning next. Being a relatively normal teen, she had actually enjoyed the thrilling and unusual rides.

She was worried about the consequences if she

and her mortal companions got caught with their hands in the leprechaun king's golden till.

Then again—

Sabrina tensed as a track resembling a dry-cleaning clothes conveyor formed overhead and clamped onto her strap. An instant later she was being whipped forward and around serpentine curves so fast, she was certain she heard a sonic boom in her wake.

☆

Chapter 13

☆

This is the end of the rainbow?" Mr. Kraft slumped. "I just stuffed my favorite tie in a cat's mouth for nothing!"

"And what were you expectin', then?" Fergus asked.

Val shrugged. "A great hall furnished with toadstools?"

"This is just another clearing in another stupid forest!" Disappointed, Libby pouted.

"Well, it's not just another clearing," Harvey said. "It's the last clearing."

"It's pretty and peaceful, though." Val withered under Libby's scathing gaze.

"Where's the gold?" Whiskers twitching, Salem scrambled up a nearby tree to get a better view.

"It's right there!" Sabrina pointed to a huge pottery crock overflowing with gold coins, jewelry, and trinkets sitting a few feet to her right. Nestled among brightly colored wildflowers on the edge of the woods, the glazed crock glistened in a shaft of sunlight.

"Oh, my!" Fergus chuckled.

"Where?" Shielding her eyes from the sun, Libby peered across the glen.

"Over here." Exasperated and tired, Sabrina stepped up to the pot. She scooped a handful of gold coins and held them up before she realized something was drastically amiss.

"Who are you?" Mr. Kraft barked at Fergus. "You're a little short for a high school student, aren't you?"

"That's Fergus, Mr. Kraft. The leprechaun." Sabrina wondered if the vice-principal was suffering from amnesia because he accidentally hit his head when the rainbow conveyor tossed them out the door.

"A leprechaun, Ms. Spellman?" Mr. Kraft scowled as he scanned the area around him. "What leprechaun?"

Libby's eyes widened with shock. "Why am I standing in a field with all you freaks?"

"Maybe we took the long way to the parade?" Val asked hopefully.

"Good. Then maybe we missed it," Harvey said.

"Wait a minute!" A twinge of panic seized Sabrina. Everyone except her was losing all memory of their rainbow adventure. "What's happening, Fergus?"

"It's the shamrock, I'm afraid. The effects are wearin' off." Fergus shrugged. "You're a witch, so the rules and regulations aren't quite the same where you're concerned. You won't be losin' your memory for one thing."

"Great!" Annoyed, Sabrina rested her foot on the edge of the crock. At least no one would remember that she was a witch. "So how am I supposed to get them home if they can't see you or the rainbow?"

"Oh, that won't be a problem a'tall!" Laughing merrily, Fergus held on to his hat as a howling wind began to blow.

Sabrina stared as a swirling whirlpool formed in the rainbow. The wind grew in intensity until one by one, Mr. Kraft, Libby, Harvey, and Val were pulled off their feet and sucked into the colorful vortex.

Yanked off the tree, Salem dug his claws into the ground, but he wasn't strong enough to counter the vacuum effect. He left tiny furrows in the dirt as the rainbow pulled, then whipped him inside. Then the whirlpool irised down to nothing and closed with a faint *pop!*

Left alone in the faery glen with Fergus, Sabrina frowned. "What about me? Am I stranded here or what?"

"No, I wouldn't be sayin' that." Whistling, Fergus idly studied a flower at his feet.

"Are you responsible for keeping me here, Fergus?"

"Come to think of it, we never did settle that little matter of the insult you did me this mornin'."

Sabrina's eyes flashed indignantly. "I just told you I thought your ancestors were great."

"Aye, but what's that to do with showin' some respect for me and the other wee folk?"

"Well, considering your roots, I can understand why you get upset when someone makes fun of you." Sabrina really did understand, but that didn't change how she felt about the leprechaun's devious methods and cunning personality.

"I see." Rocking back on his heels, Fergus mocked her with a sly grin. "So can you be swearin' on your witch's honor that you respect me, then?"

Sabrina sighed. "No."

Fergus nodded. "But you're not wantin' to be pestered with me tricks forever, either, are you?"

"Not hardly."

"Well, then, if you'd be pickin' up that crock o' gold and takin' it to me door, I'll gladly forgive and forget." When Sabrina didn't move to comply, Fergus added, "There's no other way I'll be removin' me curse. Of that you can be sure."

"All right! Why not? I'm here. Anything to get rid of you!" Exhaling in disgust, Sabrina pointed at the crock.

"Finger lift this pot of gold
and make it light for me to hold."

The heavy crock rose from the ground and
settled into Sabrina's open arms. Although she
had cast the spell, she was still surprised at how
light it was. "Cool! Now what?"

"Now we'll be arrestin' you for stealing the
king's gold!"

Sabrina glanced back to see several frowning
leprechauns standing in a semicircle behind her.
"This isn't what it looks like."

"We'll let the king be the judge of that!"

"Admit it, Hilda." Zelda gave her sister a gentle
shove, then adjusted the bodhran case slung over
her own shoulder. "You had fun."

"Yeah, I did. No musician can resist the enthusiastic applause of an audience numbering in the
hundreds." Clutching her violin case to her chest,
Hilda smiled as they entered Westbridge High and
headed for Mr. Kraft's office.

The Westbridge sidewalks had been jammed
with a cheering crowd, and this year's St. Patrick's
Day parade was being touted as the best ever.

"It's almost too bad that the mortal population
won't remember why they had such a good time
when they wake up tomorrow," Zelda said.

"Yeah, but everyone still has tonight! The
shamrock effects won't wear off for a few hours
yet." Hilda heard a loud rattling noise and looked

back. Patrick and his faery friend Edwina were shaking all the student locker doors as they passed. "I'm just grateful everyone in Westbridge is in a mood to party. I'd hate to think what might happen if the little people got bored."

"I'm not going to think about it!" Zelda rolled her eyes as she turned into the school office.

Mrs. Atherton was still behind the counter even though school had been dismissed hours ago. She held several playing cards in her hand and stared intently at the frowning leprechaun sitting cross-legged on the desk before her.

"You wouldn't be havin' some eights, now, would you?" The little man's eyes narrowed.

"Go fish!" Mrs. Atherton laughed with delight. "I'm gonna beat you this time, Michael!"

"Oh, and we'll just be seein' about that!" Michael drew from the deck, then slapped a pair of fives on the desk.

Totally engrossed in their game, neither Mrs. Atherton nor Michael looked up when Hilda's rainbow pager began to ding.

"Yes!" Hilda and Zelda charged into Mr. Kraft's office just as the colorful striped arch appeared in the corner.

"And who was daft enough to be goin' after King Kevin's pot o' gold, I'd like to know?" Patrick scowled as he and Edwina flanked the witches to greet the returning travelers.

"Do you know Fergus?" Hilda tensed as a small depression formed in the rainbow.

146

"Sure and he's a sly one, Fergus is," Edwina said.

Patrick sighed. "Aye. He's been tryin' to trick someone into gettin' old Kevin's gold for centuries."

"Fergus, mortals, and shamrock." Hilda held her breath as the rainbow puckered. "Enough said."

"Sure and that would account for it." Patrick nodded.

"Here they come!" Zelda stepped back as the rainbow suddenly spit Mr. Kraft, Libby, Harvey, Val, and Salem onto the carpeted floor.

The rainbow instantly disappeared.

"Why am I sprawled on the floor? Did we just have an earthquake?" Mr. Kraft adjusted his glasses as he got to his feet.

"I don't think so." Dazed, Harvey shook his head. "This is Massachusetts."

Since the mortals obviously didn't have a clue about where they had been, Hilda drew Salem aside and whispered. "Where's Sabrina?"

"I'm not sure, but I think she was caught red-handed dipping into King Kevin's petty cash by the palace guard."

"Oh, no." Zelda inhaled sharply.

Weaving slightly, Salem leaned against Hilda's leg for support. "Water World's Rapid Ride is flat compared to the rainbow's spiral slide."

"Keep your voice down, Salem!" Hilda hissed.

"Not necessary. Fergus gave me the power of

invisibility until midnight. Mortals who haven't eaten shamrock can't see or hear me unless I want them to."

"I strongly suggest you keep a low profile, then." Worried, Hilda turned her attention back to Sabrina. "Don't forget she's a teenager, Zelda. She can wheedle her way out of detention, household chores, and being grounded. Chances are good she can wheedle her way out of Faery Hill."

"I certainly hope you're right, Hilda."

"Why aren't you kids in class?" Wincing, Mr. Kraft moved his shoulders and arms as though he was stiff and sore all over. "I feel like I just finished running the decathlon."

"You called us into your office, Mr. Kraft." Harvey squinted, trying to remember. "Didn't he, Val?"

Val nodded slowly. "Something about a coffeehouse, wasn't it, Libby?"

"I'm not speaking to you!" An uncertain frown furrowed Libby's brow. "Although I can't remember exactly why."

"My gig!" Mr. Kraft gasped.

"Don't worry, Mr. Kraft," Zelda said. "You've still got thirty minutes to get there."

"Thirty minutes?" Mr. Kraft grabbed Zelda's arms. "I don't have my guitar! I haven't even changed! I—" He paused. "I have absolutely no idea what I've been doing all day!"

Hilda quietly pointed Mr. Kraft's guitar and

case onto the floor beside her, then pointed the rumpled vice-principal into boots, jeans, and a green shirt with a gold shamrock embroidered on the pocket. She left the top two buttons undone.

"Hey, Mr. Kraft!" Val made an OK sign with her fingers. "Sharp!"

"Come on, Willard." Hilda picked up the guitar case and shoved it into his hand. "Let's go. I've never been late for a performance, and I'm not gonna start now."

"You mean you're going to sit in with me?"

Hilda shrugged. "Why not? I just spent all afternoon brushing up on my Celtic moves."

"So did I." Mr. Kraft hesitated again. "I think."

"Me, too!" Zelda patted her bodhran case. "Working as a trio, we'll be a sensation!"

"I thought you didn't play the bodhran, Zelda." Mr. Kraft patted his pockets. "Has anyone seen my keys?"

"She's a quick study." Hilda pointed Mr. Kraft's car keys out of the pants she had deposited in his laundry basket at home and into his back pocket. Then she waved for Libby, Harvey, and Val to follow. "You, too! We're gonna need all the moral support we can get."

"Let's not forget the cat!" Salem darted for the door, singing in his human baritone. "'And we're off to Dublin in the green, in the green—'"

Hilda sighed as she closed the door behind her. On the plus side, Salem seemed to have given

149

up his aspirations to yowl in disharmony with the cat chorus that practiced in the alley. Now she just had to hope that Sabrina would soon be off to Westbridge on the rainbow, and not bound for eternal servitude in King Kevin's kitchen.

☆

Chapter 14

☆

Guilty!" Sitting on a golden throne with red velvet cushions, King Kevin shook a shillelagh at Sabrina, then setting the club aside, he held out his mug. Another leprechaun filled it with mead from a pewter pitcher, set the pitcher down, then picked up a tin whistle and started to play.

Sabrina sat in a corner of the huge castle room the wee men had carved from a mountain cavern. The hush that had fallen over the assembly of little people dissipated after the king's pronouncement, and a party atmosphere resumed. Fergus joined right in as the hall filled with laughter and music.

"Hey! What kind of trial was that?" Outraged, Sabrina stood up.

Silence settled over the hall when King Kevin

raised his shillelagh again. "A fair one and you're lucky to be havin' a trial a'tall!"

"Fair! You call that fair? I didn't even get to defend myself!"

"And what's to defend, I'd like to know?" King Kevin laughed. "You were caught holding me pot o' gold in your very own arms!"

Whistles and cheers echoed off the cavern walls.

"I know, but I wasn't holding it for me! He wanted it!" Sabrina pointed an accusing finger at Fergus.

"Sure and I did, Sabrina, me darlin'." Fergus raised his mug and grinned.

"See? He even admits it!"

"That's still no defense," King Kevin scoffed. "Of course Fergus wanted it. He's a leprechaun!"

Laughter and murmurs of assent rippled through the crowd.

"But," the king went on, "he didn't take possession of it, now, did he?"

"No." Pushing a strand of hair off her face, Sabrina sat back down and forced herself to stay calm. She had to think of something quickly if she didn't want to spend the next few centuries polishing itty-bitty cobblestones with a toothbrush. Somehow, she had to outwit the leprechaun king, a feat that had rarely, if ever, been accomplished.

She couldn't believe that Fergus was innocent of any wrongdoing just because he hadn't taken delivery of the crock! Leprechaun justice obviously had some intriguing loopholes. Which gave Sabrina a sudden inspiration.

"And how do you know I would have given it to him?" Sabrina asked.

"Meanin' that you might have tried keepin' it for yourself?" King Kevin took a long swallow of mead and smacked his lips. "Now, I don't know that and that's for sure."

"So if you don't know that"—Sabrina paused to let the suspense mount—"then you also don't know that I was plannin' to give it back. To you!"

The king laughed. "Do you think I'm daft, girl? You can't be provin' that was your intent."

"And you can't be provin' it wasn't!" Sabrina nodded emphatically. "I rest my case."

The king blinked.

A rumble of excited conversation swept through the assembly.

"Are me ears deceivin' me, or did she just outwit the king?" A little man sitting at a nearby table stared at Sabrina, amazed.

"Sure and she did, the clever girl." His companion chuckled. "Ol' Kevin can't dispute the logic of that!"

Sabrina smiled at the king. "Can I go now?"

Shaken, King Kevin eyed her warily. "And would you be thinkin' o' braggin' to anyone about how you outwitted the king of the leprechauns? We've got a reputation to consider, you know?"

Sabrina raised her hand. "On my witch's honor, I'll never say a word about it."

"Then I've no grounds to be keepin' you here, lass." Relaxing, the king raised his mug to her. "But you're welcome to stay and enjoy the hooley awhile!"

"Thanks, but no, thanks. I don't do whatever that is."

The king shook his head sadly. "Things must be fair glum in the mortal realm if there's no cause to party."

"Oh! I love to party! But the truth is I've got to go help out a friend. Well, he's not actually a friend. He's a vice-principal, which makes him the sworn enemy of every teenager everywhere. But I gave my word, so I—"

"Pssssssst."

Sabrina paused. "What, Fergus? Haven't you gotten me into enough trouble today?"

"Just a friendly word of advice," Fergus whispered. "Stop babbling and be on your way before the king changes his mind."

"Good advice. I'll take it." Sabrina looked at Fergus askance. "Why aren't you working on Aunt Hilda's boot?"

"And how will I be havin' any fun on St. Patrick's Day if I deliver that boot and settle up with Hilda?" Fergus huffed. "Besides, she's grown a wee bit fond of me over the years."

"Not!" Sabrina waved at King Kevin. "What's

the punishment for a leprechaun that gets caught and doesn't grant a legitimate wish?"

Fergus spoke before the king could respond. "Sure and you're too clever for the likes of me, Sabrina Spellman. Outwitting two leprechauns in less than five minutes! We'll just be goin' now!"

Fergus snapped his fingers.

Sabrina was whisked out of the leprechaun cavern in a cloud of golden dust. In the blink of an eye she was standing on the sidewalk outside the Coffee Mug. There was no sign of Fergus, however.

"Hey! Sabrina!" a muted voice called.

Sabrina turned to see Harvey peering through the front window. Val stood behind him, waving her to come in. Just behind Val, she could see Mr. Kraft tuning up his guitar in front of a microphone. Even more bizarre than the sight of the vice-principal preparing to make his musical debut was the sight of her aunts getting ready to join him!

Aunt Hilda, who despised Irish music, finished applying rosin to her bow and began warming up with a lively reel. Aunt Zelda, who had no interest in music beyond listening, was striking a round drum with a short stick.

"Sabrina!" Mrs. Quick stuck her head out the coffeehouse door. "Better get inside, dear. The show's about to start!"

"Thanks, Mrs. Quick." As Sabrina moved to enter, the math teacher put out a staying hand.

"Wait. Don't step on the little guys."

Sabrina waited as a faery and a leprechaun carrying a large tray of shamrock cookies scurried past her. She grabbed the door as Mrs. Quick let go.

"We were wondering what happened to you, Patrick." Mrs. Quick popped a cookie in her mouth. "Oh, that's much better. You were starting to get a teeny bit fuzzy there. And don't worry, Edwina. If you can't see, you can sit on my lap."

Shaking her head, Sabrina stepped inside. The Coffee Mug was packed with teenagers, teachers, regular patrons, and little people. Extra folding chairs had been squeezed in around all the tables, and people stood along the back wall. Fergus sat at his cobbler's bench in the coatrack alcove making Aunt Hilda's other boot. A man behind the counter wearing a "Kiss Me, I'm Irish" sweatshirt was ringing up order tickets and grinning broadly. Obviously the owner, Sabrina thought as she wove her way to the front table, where Harvey was saving her a seat.

"Glad you made it," Harvey said. "Where have you been?"

"Well—"

"You don't have to answer that." Val smiled sheepishly as Sabrina sat down. "We don't have the faintest idea where we've been all day, either!"

"You're back, Sabrina!" Aunt Zelda sat on a high stool with her foot resting on a rung and the drum resting on her leg. "You can tell us all about it on our break. Isn't this just too cool?"

"Hey, Sabrina!" Aunt Hilda smiled and waved, then turned on Mr. Kraft with a stern glare. "I don't sing, Willard. This is your gig. You start!"

"Mind if I sit on your lap?" Salem appeared between Sabrina's feet.

"Sure, Salem. Hop up. Are you visible or still cloaked?"

"Cloaked. They don't allow cats in coffee-houses." Salem snorted. "What, I ask you, is a cat who's craving mocha cappuccino with double cream supposed to do? Sheesh!"

"Salem." Harvey cocked his head thoughtfully. "He's not gonna sing or anything, is he?"

Val cuffed Harvey on the shoulder. "Cats can't sing!"

"I know." Harvey rolled his eyes. "I just don't know how I know. If that makes any sense."

Sabrina smiled as Mr. Kraft stepped up to the microphone.

The room suddenly grew quiet.

Mr. Kraft adjusted his guitar strap. Aunt Zelda raised her stick. Aunt Hilda slipped her fiddle under her chin and poised the bow over the strings.

Everyone in the audience tensed.

Mr. Kraft stared at the sea of expectant faces,

his eyes glazed with fright. Clenching her jaw, Aunt Hilda gently kicked his leg. Startled, Mr. Kraft moved his thumb across the guitar strings.

Plick. Plick. Plick. Plick.

"Oh, ye—" Mr. Kraft's voice cracked. He stopped strumming and clamped his mouth closed.

Sitting at the next table, Libby covered her eyes. "I can't watch. This is so embarrassing."

"Mr. Kraft!" Sabrina hissed, drawing his stricken gaze. "Remember Lugh of the long arm!"

Mr. Kraft hesitated, frowned slightly, then nodded. Taking a deep breath, he squared his shoulders and strummed again. "'Oh, ye bully boys of Belfast town, I'll have you to beware—'"

"Yeah!" Laughing, Sabrina shook her fist in the air and began clapping along as Mr. Kraft launched into the traditional Irish seaman's song "The Banks of Newfoundland." Aunt Zelda picked up the beat and Aunt Hilda jumped in to carry the melody on the violin. Within a few seconds everyone was clapping and singing the simple chorus.

"'And we'll rub around . . . and scrub around . . . with holey stone and saaaand—'"

Distracted by a tap on her arm, Sabrina looked down. Fergus was standing beside her. Hanging his head, he nervously shuffled his foot. "Are you finished with Aunt Hilda's second boot already?"

"No, but—I don't want to be workin' when

everyone else is havin' fun! Sure and I promise I'll finish it, though. When the band takes a break."

"Have a seat, Fergus." Grinning, Sabrina scooted over to make room for the wee man. Then she cupped her hands around her mouth and yelled. "It's a hooley!"

Author's Note

The people and situations Sabrina and her companions encounter on the rainbow ride are drawn from Celtic history and myth. For the sake of fun, the heroic tales as depicted in this book have been altered.

According to legend, Balor, the evil champion of the Fomorians, could fell a man with a mere glance. Lugh of the long arm defeated Balor by casting a stone into his eye when his eyelid drooped. Amergin, the most famous of the Celtic bards, arrived in Ireland with the Milesians and witnessed the defeat of the Tuatha De Danaan. All traces of the Danaan disappeared following the decisive battle. Making themselves invisible, the Danaan retreated underground to reign over Ireland's spiritual world. The island was called Erin, in honor of the Danaan queen, Eriu. Cuchulain, son of Lugh, defended the road to Connacht as related here. Since no one in Queen Maeve's army could duplicate Cuchulain's knotted sapling, the geis was honored. The Connacht army's advance into Ulster to steal the Brown Bull of Quelgny was delayed by a day. Fionn MacCumhail, or Finn

MacCool, successfully defended the mound of Tara from Aillen's fireballs. Wearing a cap of silence, he was not lulled to sleep by the goblin's flute and felled Aillen with a magic spear. At the age of seventeen he was appointed leader of the fianna, the king's elite guard, by Cormac MacArt.

About the Author

Diana G. Gallagher lives in Minnesota with her husband, Marty Burke, four dogs, three cats, a cranky parrot and a white rabbit. When she's not writing, she spends her time walking the dogs, pottering in the garden, playing the guitar and going to garage sales looking for cool stuff for her grandsons, Jonathan, Alan and Joseph. Diana loves Irish legends and folk music and performs at science-fiction conventions around America.

Gaze into the future and see what wonders lie in store for
Sabrina, the Teenage Witch . . .

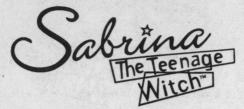

#29 Millennium Madness

Oh no! Witches have to deal with computer problems just
like mortals do, and it looks like Y2K is going to be one big
headache for Sabrina and her aunts! Something is very
wrong with the Great Clock of the Other Realm; just like
many of the computerized devices in the mortal realm,
when the New Year hits, it will stop working. Which would
cause magic everywhere to cease to exist!

As the last hours wind down, time blurs, speeds up, and
runs backwards — with some pretty embarrassing results
for Sabrina! While the Witches' Council focuses on repairing
the clock, Sabrina decides to take charge of building a
new one.

Using her now-wobbly magic, Sabrina discovers that to
build the new clock, she must collect souvenirs from twelve
magical moments in history. Will she complete her
scavenger hunt in time to save the Other Realm?

Don't miss out on any of Sabrina's magical antics — conjure up
a book from the past for a truly spellbinding read . . .

#18 I'll Zap Manhattan

So Circe is a few thousand years old and used to hang
around with the Greek gods. Does that give her the right
to spoil everyone's fun at a Witches' Council dance?
Sabrina doesn't think so. She ruins Circe's night instead.
No big deal, right?

Wrong. Circe is peeved! And she knows just how to get back
at Sabrina: kidnap Harvey. Before long he's trapped in
Circe's pocket world — a twisted version of Manhattan —
wearing a toga and feeding Circe grapes. Even worse,
Circe can't resist turning men into swine, and Harvey
could be next . . .

This is no future for the guy Sabrina loves! But how can her
puny magic beat one of the most powerful sourceresses of
all time?